THE STORY GOES THIS WAY

A COLLECTION OF SHORT STORIES

ANOOP K NAIR

Copyright © Anoop K Nair
All Rights Reserved.

This book has been self-published with all reasonable efforts taken to make the material error-free by the author. No part of this book shall be used, reproduced in any manner whatsoever without written permission from the author, except in the case of brief quotations embodied in critical articles and reviews.

The Author of this book is solely responsible and liable for its content including but not limited to the views, representations, descriptions, statements, information, opinions and references ["Content"]. The Content of this book shall not constitute or be construed or deemed to reflect the opinion or expression of the Publisher or Editor. Neither the Publisher nor Editor endorse or approve the Content of this book or guarantee the reliability, accuracy or completeness of the Content published herein and do not make any representations or warranties of any kind, express or implied, including but not limited to the implied warranties of merchantability, fitness for a particular purpose. The Publisher and Editor shall not be liable whatsoever for any errors, omissions, whether such errors or omissions result from negligence, accident, or any other cause or claims for loss or damages of any kind, including without limitation, indirect or consequential loss or damage arising out of use, inability to use, or about the reliability, accuracy or sufficiency of the information contained in this book.

Made with ♥ on the Notion Press Platform
www.notionpress.com

To You, Dear Reader,

for making this journey worthwhile.

For every reader who finds a piece of themselves within
these chapters

Contents

For the Magic of Story telling, an eternal flame

1

SCAR CITY

The evolution of mankind has been one of the greatest blessings for us. Unlike other species, the quest to achieve something in life is what keeps us going. This is the tale of two such cities, which progressed rapidly over a period of time. One of the cities, Orizon, was rich in natural resources like minerals, oil, and energy, and also thrived in agriculture, while the other city, Stilon, was rich in knowledge and history. Earlier, these two cities were like brothers in arms, very close and always helping each other. With time, the people of Stilon became more educated and moved to different parts of the world. Some of them became merchants and successful entrepreneurs worldwide. They flourished in academics, finance, research, health, science, and technology and made a name for themselves. On the other hand, Orizon concentrated on cultivating its natural resources, and the people there were very hard-working but less educated than those of Stilon. As both these small cities were neighbours, most of the resources of Orizon had been shared with Stilon since old times. Stilon did not have to look beyond Orizon to meet the city's basic needs. Slowly, the city of Stilon started advancing and began importing raw materials and goods from other cities as they were cheaper. They did not realise that they were of inferior quality.

During those times, Orizon was going through a rough patch. An ongoing drought took a toll on the region; people were dying of hunger and thirst. There were no labourers to do any work. Mining went for a toss due to the impending dry spell; agriculture was impacted, and the region slumped into poverty. Some of the people there stooped to robbery to meet their ends. The city thought that Stilon would help them in this crisis. The older generation of people living in Stilon urged the younger generation to help their neighbouring city. Even though Stilon had the technology, resources, and skillset to easily help and eliminate the problems of their neighbour, they turned their backs on them. They did not have the gratitude to thank their neighbours for what they were today, thanks to the goodwill gesture of Orizon back then.

One day, suddenly all the people in Stilon started getting scars on their bodies and faces. The people of Stilon could not travel to other parts of the world, as the other cities thought this was an infectious disease that could spread rapidly worldwide. So they isolated the people of Stilon and curbed their travel. The merchants could not trade. The scientists were banned from attending conventions across the world. The doctors, who themselves had scars, could not attend to other patients and as they could not cure themselves, people worldwide lost their faith in them. Everything came to a standstill in Stilon. The people of Stilon did not have any other skills that they could utilise and their daily bread and butter was affected. The Red Cross and other medical agencies arranged food and blankets for the people. Their doctors worked day in and day out to treat the scars, but their efforts were all in vain. When nothing worked, they called the Saints from Vatican City. The priests sprinkled holy water on the faces of citizens and blessed them. During all this time, no one bothered about Orizon, as this city was relatively lesser known to other regions of the world. Their suffering largely continued.

While all this was going on, an old farmer from Orizon came one day to meet his son who was a citizen of Stilon and was suffering from the same scars that the whole city was facing then. The farmer dad had educated his son, who became a famous scientist. Even though the scientist son remained busy and only went to visit his parents once in a while, his father, who loved his son very much, went to Stilon, despite knowing that the people there were infected by an unknown disease. His son warned him not to come in close contact with him, to which the farmer dad said he was going through the worst already and did not have any more fear. His son told him about the state of Stilon, how everyone was trying to help them, including the doctors from other parts of the world, charity institutions who were giving them donations to tackle the problems of the people, and the priests who came all the way from Vatican and other cities to bless them in these dark times. His dad laughed on hearing this. He asked his son a question and asked him to reply to that question in just a single word. The question was 'Tell me a single word that best describes the current state of the region where we reside in'. His son attempted and gave various answers like drought, misery, etc., but none of them was the right answer. The farmer dad gave him some medicines that he got from his hometown before finally giving him a hug. He said the answer to all the problems of the city lay in that single word that his father was expecting from him. He then bid him farewell and left. The son kept thinking and then finally came to a word that had not struck him before.

He instantly got up from bed and strode outside in his pajamas shouting 'Eureka, Eureka'. He got into his car and drove across to the government headquarters, wanting to meet the prime minister. As the scientist's son was famous and was acquainted with major influential people across the city, the prime minister instantly met him. There was a closed group discussion with some other members.

Soon after the meeting, the scientist formed a panel of technology experts, agriculture research institute members, and other prominent people, and from there went on a high-level delegation to Orizon.

This delegation panel discussed with the people of Orizon and imparted some techniques and methods to adopt in the next few months, which included cloud seeding. A few months later, it rained in Orizon. Once again, the farmers got back into their occupation and the labourers started working everywhere.

Slowly Orizon came back to its old state and once again became a reservoir of natural resources. The people of Orizon thanked the scientist and his group of experts from all their hearts for solving their problems. Every one of them became happy again.

The scientist returned to Stilon in the evening. He had tears of joy while going back; those tears were for a significant accomplishment. That night he slept well. The next morning he was brushing his teeth when he glanced at the mirror. What he saw startled him. All the scars on his body and face had gone. He was overjoyed and came running out of the bathroom. He saw that his wife and kids also lost their scars and were smiling back at him. When he looked out the window, the entire city was dancing in joy. The deadly infection had vanished overnight, and people were cured automatically.

His father, on hearing the good news, came to meet him. The son thanked him for making him realise his mistake and giving this city a second chance. When his father asked him if he got the one-word answer to his question that he asked him when they met last time, he said yes. The word was 'Scarcity'. That was the state of Orizon when he came to meet his son, and the father correlated that word beautifully with the state of Stilon, which was **Scar City**. Instantly, the son realised it was his duty to help the people of Orizon, and this is how the problems of both the cities came to an end...

2

THE OFFERING

The drums started playing. Fires were lit for the holy day. Ryan was just 6 years old sitting beside his grandparents watching the ceremony. This was the first time he was allowed to see. A young boy aged 12 years was brought out of the cave. His hands and legs were tied to wooden logs. He was taken to the far side of the forest where it was dark and tied to a large boulder. Everyone dispersed from the site soon after. Ryan was curious to know what happened to the boy, but he was not allowed to know that. What he did know was that the 12 year old boy was aware of where he was being taken to and appeared to be brave enough.

While Ryan's grandparents were returning back, Ryan slowly sneaked back to the spot to see what happened to the boy. There from a distance he saw the boy was weeping silently & Ryan was surprised to still find him there. Ryan was trying to approach the boy from a distance after waving his hands to him first. But the boy gave a warning sign to Ryan to return back. Just then Ryan saw a huge shadow looming over the boy from behind. To his disbelief, he saw a mammoth lion emerge behind and snatched the boy & offthe boy disappeared. Ryan was shocked and scared on seeing this. At the same time, he heard his grandpa calling out to him. Grandpa got worried on seeing that Ryan had witnessed the final event of the ceremony: The Offering. Ryan had not only broken the rules of the tribe but had witnessed an age-old custom. Once he was back in his tent, Ryan was warned not to tell this to anyone. Or else he would be abandoned by the tribe.

The entire night Ryan kept thinking. Many questions came to his mind. He wondered why the tribe had only a majority of old people. Where were the small kids disappearing? Why were the women not allowed to be part of the ceremony, and most of all, why were all women in the tribe being worshipped as goddesses? He had many questions in mind and knew he should find out the answers before time runs out. In this part of the Stone Age, he knew one thing for sure: The ancient custom could not be broken. He also knew someday it would be his turn, just like the old boy, he had to train his mind and body. Then he got the answer to all his questions.

Better to hunt the beast before it hunted him.

Although there were restrictions in the tribe not to venture deep into the forest and be home before sunset, Ryan saw kids were confined to their houses and no one paid much attention to them. Rather, kids were too afraid to venture out in fear of the beast. Ryan was far ahead of other kids in strength and spirit, and this was his only chance in a lifetime to prove himself.

Every day, Ryan would get up early in the morning and accompany his grandparents to the forest to collect wood for the fires and gather fruits from the forest, which the tribe normally consumed as food. Additionally, the tribe used to hunt small animals like rabbits and boars, which they also consumed as food. While his grandparents worked, he would cut wood and sharpen them to make weapons. He secretly hid his weapons beneath the huge stone statue of Simha near the temple. It looked like he was giving the weapons as an offering to the Holy Simha. He began venturing deeper into the valleys in his mystical search for strength. He began marking the stones so that he would remember the path. *He would close his eyes and sit in a yogic position to absorb more light from the sun, sensing an inner strength.* One day, he observed some carvings on a stone of men with weapons in their hands in different poses and tried to emulate them. He studied the poses minutely and practised the art with the wooden weapons he created for himself. He practiced this for 4 to 5 years, not even realizing how much time had passed. He gained enough strength that he could now fight like a warrior.

He then started following paw prints of the beast. He had grown big enough now, and his grandparents had lifted all the restrictions, perhaps wanting him to live life fully before his turn to be offered to the beast came. What they didn't realise is the hunter was now the hunted. His movements were sharp and flexible. He had gained the language of animals' voices and knew their exact meaning by now during his visits to the jungle. It was time now for the bait. He hunted a deer& tied it to the strong roots of a tree and left it bleeding for the beast to smell the blood to invite him over. The Beast in fact came, but it failed to sense the danger surrounding it, which came to him as a surprise. An arrow shot from the bushes, piercing its eyes. Out of pain, the beast growled. Then Ryan pounced on the beast from the top of cliff and used a herculean club to smash its head. The growl of the beast alerted the other lions, and they came to know someone stronger than them had emerged in the jungle. He carried the beast's mane and tied it to his chest. On returning home, his tribe asked him where he got that, and he just said that he spotted it near the river. This mane had the blood of the beast engraved in it. Ryan thought he had hunted a huge beast, but the icing on the cake was that he didn't realise it was the king of all beasts. When the king gets killed, his subordinates know there is a threat to their lives too.

Meanwhile, preparations were underway for the offering on the holy day. Ryan realised it was his turn. From a fortnight back, he was being fed a lot of food. He knew this was not for him it was only to make him more fleshy for the lion's meal. On the day of the offering, Ryan was not allowed to meet his mother. He completed all the rites and rituals from the early morning. At the end of the day, just like an old boy, he was tied to logs over the body and taken to the sacred spot. His grandparents were also witnessing all this. As this was an age-old ritual, maybe there were no feelings or emotions left with the tribe while parting with their young ones. Ryan was pierced with a piece of wood inside his mouth so that he would not shout on seeing the lion, as sometimes the beast gets distracted on hearing the boy's sound and probably could get diverted to the old tribe which it then starts hunting.

Just like other boys, Ryan stood there waiting for his turn for the offering. But he was strong-willed and knew exactly what he wanted. Out of the darkness emerged three large beasts and started staring at the young boy. They saw the mane of the king lion on the boy's chest and realised this was the same boy. The boy, in turn, stared at the beasts and laughed at them. They bowed down to him, each one of them, and sat there for the rest of the night protecting their new King.

In the morning, when the tribe woke up and thought of cleaning the place that would be filled with blood and bones, they saw the boy sitting right there surrounded and guarded by lions, much to their dismay. They removed the wooden block from his throat and took him out of the place. Ryan then asked the lions to feast on the tribe and the beasts attacked and killed all the members in the tribe except the young children. Ryan had signalled the lions not to touch the young boys. After this, the lions bowed to him and left the place. Ryan went back to the cave where other ladies, and children were confined. He explained the entire story to them and then led them all far away.

3

THE DARK BLESSING

Clive was the ideal role model for all ambitious youngsters of his age. Just at the age of 27 years, he was well placed with a leading financial organisation. A banker by profession, Clive's job was to analyse the trends in the financial market, to keep a tab on stock prices, and to take care of his company's investments. He drew a fat paycheck in return, and had a lush green seafront villa provided as company accommodation. It was a dream for someone his age to acquire so much in such a short time. Most of the time, he was preoccupied with meetings.

During one such crucial meeting, he took a small break and headed straight to the parking lobby. He flicked a cigarette from a pack that he used to carefully hide in his suit pocket and started smoking. Clive had started smoking right since his college days. During those days, he used to finish 2 packs a day.

Gradually this increased to 4 packs. Today the situation was so bad that he could not keep away from his best friend for a single day. Now it was like a stress buster for him.

One fine Sunday morning, he went out for a morning jog. It was a hot, sultry day. After his session, he grabbed a copy of 'The Awakening' from a nearby stall and relaxed on a bench in Paradise Park. The park was filled with people of all ages who used to come here for a breath of fresh air. With a cigarette clasped in his hands, he started browsing through news, starting with the stock market news and then gradually shifting his focus to the latest events. One such article grabbed his attention. He started reading it.

Daniel was a farmer who lived in the countryside of South Hill... The town is an outdoor lover's paradise surrounded by pine forests and the gently rolling hills of southern Virginia. South Hill traces its history back to the early 19th century. In that period, South Hill was an agrarian economy, with tobacco as the main crop. During those times, Daniel's father purchased some 56 acres of land for tobacco farming. Tobacco warehouses were established on outskirts of the farm.

More than 1.6 million pounds of tobacco were sold after the first yield. Tobacco farms had played an important role in the history of South Hill and in the tobacco industry in general. Daniel took care of the farms after his father passed away. But by then his farm had expanded in leaps and bounds, so he had to hire a few village men to take care of various chores at his farm.

Daniel led a happy, peaceful life with his wife and 2 teenage sons at South Hill. There was one person he had known since his childhood days, Dr. Williams.

Dr. Williams was a general practitioner. He was a close friend of Daniel's father. He and Daniel's father grew up together before eventually Williams went to town to pursue a career in Medicine. He was still in touch with them and they used to spend time together during weekends. It was Williams who helped Daniel look after his Dad's tobacco estate at the ripe age of 21 years. Williams had a grown-up son who was in high school. His name was Ken.

Sometimes he used to accompany his father to Daniel's estate. Williams was a very carefree person and he brought up his son in the same way. So it was surprising to see him one fine evening extremely dejected when he came to Daniel's place. When asked if something was wrong, Williams refused to answer. Instead, he asked Daniel to accompany him the next day to Williams' place. Sensing that something was wrong, Daniel agreed.

The next morning, they started. Williams was silent throughout the journey. He said that he had to attend to one of his patients at his health centre and asked me to accompany him. When they reached, Williams took Daniel straight to the second floor, room no. 609. There Daniel could see a familiar person lying on the bed. It was Ken.

After a long pause right since the early journey, Williams uttered, "Ken is suffering from blood cancer." Daniel was taken aback by his words. On seeing this,

Williams commented, "It's too late now. If only I had known that my son is addicted to smoking, maybe I would have stopped him and made him understand." Saying this, Williams put his head on Daniel's shoulders and cried incessantly. Daniel left the hospital and reached his home late at night. All through the night, he could not sleep.

The following morning, it was utter chaos in Daniel's estate. People from the nearby village were trying to douse the flames that were cast on the tobacco crops. The entire farmland was blazing in fire. All the tobacco crops were damaged. No one knew what had happened except Daniel. Daniel had realised that all through the ages Daniel's family was harvesting a killer crop. What was a blessing for his family was in turn a curse for others. Unable to see any other person going through the same situation as Ken, Daniel took a harsh decision. That night he set the tobacco estate on fire.

One of the village men tried to stop him too, but he never gave up. The next morning the entire village came to know of this incident through that village man who saw the entire episode. People started thinking that Daniel was out of his mind. They started cursing Daniel and his family. Daniel was unable to take up all the pain and realised that it was good to end up their lives. All this while Williams was still consoling his son's death when suddenly he came to know of the events at South Hill. He immediately started for South Hill. But on reaching there he was shocked. The bodies of Daniel Dsouza and his family were already being taken for cremation. Williams was shocked.

It was 11 March 09, No Tobacco Day! Clive was about to finish the article written by Dr. Williams in honour of his dear friend, Daniel. As he finished the article, he dropped the cigarette from his hand. He knew he did not have such a bad choice as that of Daniel and vowed never to touch the deadly thing ever again.

4

THE SAINT AND THE SINNER

"**D**ehradun – The dream destination in the Doon Valley." Set amidst the Himalayas, Shivaliks, Ganges, and Yamuna, Dehradun is indeed a picture-perfect hill resort. I sat on the bus recollecting what my father had told me when I was just 7 years old, that he wanted to see me grow up here. It was his dream to see me as a commanding officer graduating from the Indian Military Academy, Dehradun. And today, after 24 long years, when I saw my bus passing by IMA, Dehradun, those memories struck me.

As I grew up, I realised that I would not be able to adhere to the strict disciplinary rules that are followed in the army. I was a rebel right from my childhood days. Though I loved rifle shooting and always accompanied my father on his hunting expeditions, it was not my desire to join the Army.

Rather, I wanted to be a sportsman in the game of rifle shooting. But when I took the test, they declared that my eyesight was not perfect, especially for this kind of sport as I had a minor cylindrical number in my left eye. Well, things never happened as per my expectations.

The bus came to a grinding halt. Suddenly, I came back to my senses. A shepherd was crossing the street with his herd of sheep. Reclining onto the couch, I sat listening to my favourite melodies on my iPod. I glanced across the sky and found misty clouds descending on the valley, and could sense the cold air around it. The roads in this valley were approximately 120 feet above sea level right on the hilly slopes. I was appreciating the driving skills of these daredevil drivers when my bus negotiated a deadly turn on a downhill road. The bus driver did not realise that a water tanker from the opposite end was about to accelerate towards the gradient. As he tried to avert the crash by turning away and applying the brakes consequently, he failed in his judgement and our bus started rolling down the ravine.

I could hear the cries of children on the bus but to no avail. I tried to grab a thick branch of a tree that was hanging down from what seemed to me like a narrow opening of a cave. Fortunately, I was in the window seat of the bus through which I could escape and hold that branch before the bus took its final leap down the valley. I eventually succeeded in gaining my balance but could not hold onto my shoulder bag, which fell off my shoulders. When I looked down, everything had vanished into thin air. I didn't know how I survived.

I slowly started climbing the slope along with the support of rocks; I could see a *jhola* lying near the crevice of a sharp rock. I took that *jhola*, expecting to find something that I could bank on for the rest of my journey. I finally managed to reach the hill road, but my arms were bruised, and my knees were bleeding. Blood was oozing out of my calf muscle, which had torn during the accident. Estimating that I would find a piece of cloth to tighten around my calf muscle, I was about to open the *jhola*. Just then I heard a voice from somewhere. 'Son, what are you doing here, and from where did you get my bag?'

After the accident, my vision had gone blurred. I could sense that a pale-looking man with a thick, long beard was standing next to me. But I was not able to contemplate the reason for his strange appearance at that instant.

I said, 'Guruji, my bus met with an accident. Ironically, I am the only survivor. I have lost all my belongings and am in deep pain. I was searching for something that could heal my wound, and for that reason, I tried to open your *jhola*.'

'Son, may I know the purpose of your visit to this place?' asked the saint.

'I like going places; I am a vagabond,' I said.

'What's your profession?' queried the Saint.

'I help people fulfil their ends of living,' I said.

'You mean to say that you are a philanthropist,' said the saint.

'Yeah, something like that,' I proclaimed.

'Have you committed any sins in your life?' asked the Saint.

'No!' came the stark reply from me.

'No one is clean, son; I believe people come here to wash their sins in the holy waters of the Ganges, which is just a few miles from here. If you wish to accompany me, you can,' said the saint.

I had heard that Dehradun is the gateway to many other places of tourist interest like Haridwar, Rishikesh, Badrinath, Kedarnath, Gangotri, and Yamunotri, etc.

'As darkness was about to fall, I realised this was the only option I had on that fateful evening. I did not want to be lost somewhere in this desolate place.'

As I started walking along, this saint, who almost sounded like my father, was trying to get every detail of my life right from my schooling days until today.

After a brief discussion, this saint asked me, "Till now, you have lied about everything to me. And you say you are clean?"

"What have I lied to you?" I asked gently, trying to control my anger.

"Everything, except those that you told about your childhood days," said the saint sternly.

"You had a fascination for hunting, just like your father. You thought that you could be like your father, but strangely as you grew up, your differences with your father also widened. You left your home to prove something, but when you failed, you knew you couldn't make it back. That's what forced you to take up this job."

"I admit that you like to go places, but that is because you have a mission - a task to fulfill, in each place you go, that's how you are here, my son," said the saint firmly.

Before he could add further, I interrupted, "Yeah, I am a professional assassin and sharpshooter and presently am on the run. I thought this could be the best place for cover."

"You cannot fool a nobleman," said the saint.

"But it was you who told me that no one is clean, isn't it? That means you too came here with an intention – the intention of running away from your past." I asked.

"Yes," came the reply, and as these words echoed in my ears and faded forever,

I opened that *jhola* and took out the saffron robes of the saint from the bag and stood behind a tree and wore them. I also disguised myself with a long artificial beard that I found in the bag. I knew I had to stay away from the long hands of the law for quite some time and this was the best way I could.

I also knew that habits die hard and thought the best way to stay away was to adopt another bad habit. The search was not long before I spotted a hookah in that *jhola.* These saints normally resort to smoking hookah, which is an intoxicant that gives a soothing feeling to your nerves and transports you to a different world, commonly referred to as 'Moksha'.

Today as I lie meditating on the banks of the Ganges, I have won a thousand followers. I can still recollect that fateful evening when I encountered my alter ego - the saint. I have stopped killing people; rather, I bless them these days for their long life. Today, I also enjoy my freedom, as in my previous days. I make my own rules, but the only difference this time is that I preach them too. After listening to my discourses, my followers feel connected to the divine, but what they do not realise is that

"The only difference between a saint and a sinner is that a saint has a past while a sinner has a future."

5

VAGABOND

The young falcon, Walter, laid his head on his mother's lap and said, "What if I could never find my way back home again?" The mother replied, "Don't worry; you will." This is the story of the falcon who was so attached to his parents that he never flew alone. The other falcons made fun of him, but still, it did not bother Walter.

So, one day, his father, determined to make him independent, laid down a condition: "Tomorrow we will fly to the end of the mountains together, but you will have to find your way back alone. I will go ahead to hunt some shorebirds and cross the mountains. No matter what happens, don't be scared."

Thus, the father and son set out on a journey together, as the father wanted to teach his son to fly alone. The sky was clear that day, and the clouds hid behind the mountains. Walter kept talking to his dad along the way. His dad warned him not to lose sight of the track.

When they reached the mountains, the father bid his son goodbye and asked him to return home. He told his son that if he could find his way back, he would have the chance to fly with his parents forever. This was a crucial test for him. The young falcon was very scared when his father left him. He had never flown alone. Somehow, he started back, unsure of whether he would find his way.

The scorching heat of the sun began to weigh on him. He saw, far across the sky, a storm looming. He wanted to get away from the storm as soon as possible. After flying for a while, he spotted a group of birds flying together, and they waved at him to join them. Without a second thought, he sped across to them. He made some friends, and they kept wandering here and there in flocks. They then rested in the shallow branches of trees in the deep forest that evening. They had their share of food for that evening, and he saw the night unfold into a mystical scene.

The night sky lit up with stars he had never seen before, as he always reached home and went to bed early at night with his parents. All this seemed magical to him! He started realizing that he was slowly losing all his fear.

On the way back in the morning, he crossed his home and saw his mother from a distance, but this time he didn't go there. He was enjoying this new phase of his life, feeling like an explorer wanting to discover more. The same sky, which he had previously found daunting to fly alone in, now became his abode. Thus, the young falcon became courageous enough to fly without his parents.

When he grew up, he knew every corner of the sky. Most importantly, he did not feel the need to build a home, even though he laid eyes on a beautiful peregrine falcon, who, just like him, wandered in oblivion. Although he went home to meet his parents occasionally, he told them that he had found his true home—something that did not have walls or boundaries.

We all are confined within boundaries when we get a new home or a vehicle. No doubt we feel solace in our homes, or maybe we drive around within some distance, but then these assets become our limitations, and somehow, we forget that we have a beautiful world out there to explore and acclimatize to, without the need to own things that make us feel worthless, constantly fearing about repayments.

The young falcon taught me that day: Be brave and leave behind things or people that hold you back. Even if you own them, they will always be there for you. The simple things in life are what make it beautiful. Let's be vagabonds!

6

THE ANTIQUE

Mr. Sorabjee was gazing at his most prized possession one day. It was an antique brass lamp carved with precious gems. His grandson came over and asked, "What are you looking at, Grandpa?" His grandpa replied, "This brass lamp has been valuable since time immemorial." After this, he narrated a story about it.

When Mr. Sorabjee was a kid, his father got this brass lamp from Persia. At that time, Persia was known for such unique artware. His father, Mr. Dadabuoy, was a renowned industrialist. Mr. Dadabuoy was a kind-hearted and hard-working person.

At a time when the British were ruling our country, his significant contributions to the economy were indeed noteworthy. He empowered thousands of youngsters to study hard and become businessmen like him. His industries employed thousands of workers, thus providing jobs at a time when many people were starving and did not have work.

But everyone has to go through some struggles in life, and so did Dadabuoy. In his late thirties, Dadabuoy was diagnosed with a rare muscle disorder that paralyzed his arms. For treatment, he had to go to America and stay there for a couple of years.

Upon returning to India, he was shocked to see that his empire was on the verge of collapse. Some miscreants had caused rifts within the factory unions, thereby halting production. Once he came back, it took time for him to resolve these issues. But all of this incurred a lot of debts, and repayments were not possible in a short period.

Mr. Dadabuoy then decided to auction his prized possessions. On the day of the auction, he put up all his assets: his vintage motor car, the gramophone that he was hooked on in the evenings, and his most cherished brass lamp. One of the participants in the auction, Mr. Shyamlal, purchased the brass lamp for 50,000 rupees, which at that time was a huge amount. Mr. Dadabuoy didn't actually want to sell it initially, but the urge to get started again made him do so.

After several years, Mr. Dadabuoy not only bounced back from bankruptcy but also propelled his empire to new heights. He diversified his businesses and started his own five-star hotels, retail ventures, etc., to name a few. He ensured that what he took from society was always returned by starting hospitals and educational institutions. But despite all his achievements, he still regretted the fact that he had to give up his prized possessions.

One day, he divulged this in an interview with the media. As he grew old, his son Sorabjee started taking care of the businesses, including the hotel chains. Dadabuoy began to lead a retired life, spending most of his time visiting orphanages and old age homes, lending his support even at this age. He was truly an icon and an inspiration.

On the 25th anniversary of the grand five-star hotel he built, he decided to pay a visit there. After meeting the guests who had come, he sat down on the reception couch for a while. His son was busy making arrangements for the evening. Mr. Dadabuoy's attention turned toward the enclosure just behind the wall facing him. Inside the enclosure, he saw something that was familiar to him.

It was the brass lamp that had been auctioned years ago. When his son came and sat beside him, he asked how the brass lamp, which was sold years back, ended up there. His son said that someone by the name of Mr. Shyamlal had gifted it to the restaurant. There was something engraved on a golden plate just below the lamp. It read: "This is a token of gratitude to my role model, who encouraged me to be the person I am today."

It is so strange that some people come into your life as angels and help you when you need them most, just because you were an inspiration to that person someday. It was truly generous of Mr. Shyamlal to first buy the antique brass lamp from Mr. Dadabuoy at a time when it was necessary and then return it to him as a gift.

Mr. Shyamlal was on the guest list that evening, and they both met once more. They exchanged pleasantries and memories that dated back years.

7

SHRAVAN AND HIS BLIND PARENTS

We have all heard the famous story of the virtuous boy Shravan, who took care of his blind parents in ancient times and how he was accidentally killed by King Dasharatha. The king was cursed for this deed. Now, let me narrate the story of the modern-day Shravan.

Shravan was born into a middle-class family, and both his parents were blind. When Shravan was small, he used to help his mother with all the household chores. His mother felt proud of him. His father was a retired teacher who excelled in his studies, particularly in math. All his school teachers knew the circumstances surrounding Shravan and encouraged him to continue working hard in his studies.

However, he did not lead a normal life like other kids. He hardly had time to play with others his age, let alone mingle. As he grew up, his ailing parents were not in a position to do anything for themselves or for Shravan.

To add to his woes, their health condition deteriorated. He left school midway as he could not devote time to his studies. He started doing odd part-time jobs to sustain a living and look after his parents. He was so attached to them that they began to depend on him fully. Time flew by, and Shravan was now a teenager. His reclusive attitude over the years cost him his social life.

One day, his parents expressed their wish to go to Haridwar. Shravan was an obedient son, and he could not say no. Though he started planning for the trip, he was unsure if he should take them, considering their situation. But such was his dedication to them that he thought, come what may, he would oblige and fulfill his parents' wish.

One day, he went to the bank to withdraw some cash to arrange for the trip and was waiting in a queue. Suddenly, a group of robbers sneaked into the bank and ordered everyone to bend down at gunpoint. Shravan, upon seeing this, wanted to retaliate but noticed that a couple of policemen were waiting outside for the robbers to exit the bank so they could nab them red-handed. They had received a tip-off. So, he waited patiently until the robbers had their share of cash packed into bags.

Before leaving, the robbers warned the visitors in the bank not to inform anyone. As soon as they stepped out of the bank, the policemen nabbed them. Suddenly, there was a confrontation between the two police officers, as one of them was corrupt. Seeing this, one of the robbers tried to snatch a bag and run. Somehow, the honest officer managed to bring down the corrupt cop and got him handcuffed.

Meanwhile, the honest police officer started chasing the robber. Shravan knew it was hard-working men's money that was being taken away, and moreover, he wanted to arrange the cash that day itself to book tickets for his parents. So he started chasing the robber too.

Suddenly, he heard gunshots in the air just as he was within reach of the robber, and the next moment, Shravan fell to the ground, hit by a bullet from the honest police officer's gun. The policeman continued to pursue the robber, jumping and nabbing him. A couple of passers-by helped the police and confined the robber in a corner, preventing his escape. The honest police officer then came back to Shravan to check on him. Seeing Shravan severely injured, he called for an ambulance. He regretted his mistake of shooting Shravan. But Shravan stopped him from feeling remorseful. When the police officer asked why, he said that whatever the police did was a good deed. Shravan explained that he had given up his dreams of pursuing academics for the sake of his blind parents. He had taken care of them his entire life, compromising his own aspirations for theirs. So even if his life were to end, he was not regretting it, as according to him, his life had already ended when he gave up all that he wanted to achieve.

He told the police officer to arrange tickets for his parents' journey and asked him not to go visit them to deliver the bad news of their son's death, nor to tell them the actual story. He didn't want them to curse the police officer after hearing such sad news. The police officer did exactly as told and informed the media that a brave young boy had given up his life to save the hard-earned money of thousands of people and to fulfill his parents' dream. The police department arranged full-time help for his parents and provided them with a handsome compensation. The police officer was also recognized for his bravery and received a promotion.

Here, unlike King Dasharatha, who suffered pain and agony after being cursed by old Shravan's parents, the police officer lived a happy, prosperous life. He felt no guilt either, as Shravan had told him he had done a good deed by ending his life. Shravan's parents were initially upset by their son's demise, but they now had a savings account with sufficient money to spend the remainder of their lives comfortably, thanks to their son's bravery, and they eventually went to Haridwar with the assistance of domestic help. See the irony?

Last but not least, Shravan, although unhappy in his life, did not show it to anyone, including his parents. He held a secret desire within him, subdued his inner pain, and somehow felt that all this had to end. Finally, his wish was fulfilled. Even though he breathed his last, he ensured that his parents would be well taken care of even without him. It was a win-win situation for all of them at the cost of Shravan's life.

8

DISCIPLES ALIKE

Once upon a time, there was a mighty king who had a young son, his rightful heir to the throne. The young prince was brave like his father. He had many friends his age; some were children of the courtiers and ministers. Whenever the young prince did something, his friends openly shared their views and told him if they felt what he was doing was not right. However, the prince never trusted their abilities and believed that he was wise enough to make decisions on his own.

One day, the king sent him to a hermit in the forest. The king wanted him to learn from the hermit. The hermit taught him many things. Among the hermit's disciples were many others—some were blind, some were deaf, and some were very poor. But the hermit treated them all equally, regardless of the social status they belonged to or their physical abilities. This irked the prince, who thought he was superior and the most capable among them all.

On the final day of learning, the hermit gave them a test. The test was to wander and survive inside the jungle for two whole days. The young prince was confident he would pass the test with flying colors. However, the hermit formed groups of three to go together. The prince waited for the hermit to form his group. When a blind and a deaf disciple came and stood beside him, he was surprised. Despite the unusual group formation, he was undeterred and ventured into the deep jungle.

They formed a chain-like formation, with the blind person in the middle, the deaf in the front, and the prince behind them like a shadow. They held a common long stick to stay together. As they ventured deeper into the jungle, they became cautious. The young prince thought it was his responsibility to protect the other two and was extra careful as they trod the path. While crossing a bush, the blind boy suddenly asked the other two to stop and remain still. The prince and the deaf boy didn't understand why.

After a while, they saw a long, poisonous snake slither down from the bush and crawl into a burrow in search of food. The prince was astonished to realize that the blind boy had sharp hearing. Even though the prince had been extremely alert, he hadn't heard the snake's rattling. Grateful, he thanked the blind boy, and they continued on.

They traveled a couple of kilometers when the deaf boy suddenly asked them to stop. When the prince inquired why, the deaf boy urged them to concentrate on the smell in the air. The other two didn't notice anything unusual. The deaf boy then explained that he could smell fresh blood, which meant there was a predator nearby, and if they crossed its path, the predator might come after them. They decided to wait. After some time, the deaf boy signaled that it was safe to proceed.

As they walked a few more meters, they came across a carcass, reduced to bones. They realized a wild animal must have hunted and feasted on it. The prince, once again, was flummoxed by the abilities of his companions.

They decided to follow the river to quench their thirst. Upon spotting the river, the prince dashed toward it, but the deaf boy quickly alerted him to stop—there was a crocodile perched on a rock near where the prince was headed. The prince stopped and squinted at the rock, unable to spot the crocodile at first, as it was well-camouflaged. Only when it moved its leg did he see it. They went to the opposite side of the river to drink and then started their way back to the hermitage.

Upon returning, the hermit asked the prince how his experience had been. The young prince replied that it had been an eye-opening and valuable learning experience. The hermit then told him that one day, when he became king, he would encounter many people, including ministers, courtiers, and servants. On that day, he should give them all equal opportunity and freedom to make decisions, as their advice could benefit the kingdom in the long run. He should listen to their views and trust their abilities, no matter their background. The young prince truly understood and learned an important life lesson.

9

THE DWELLING

It was an exciting new day for the Mehtas. They were planning to move to a new house. After an extended search, Mr. Mehta finally decided on this house. It was located far off in the countryside, surrounded by greenery. Nearby, there was a lake where one could go fishing. Mr. Mehta was eager to see how his young children would react to the new place, as they had been living in a crowded city and were tired of the constant noise. Meanwhile, the new house had a history of its own. It had been uninhabited for around 28 years, so it had to be renovated from scratch. Mr. Mehta had recently taken up a consulting job, which allowed him to work remotely. On days when he had meetings, he would stay in town, as the new house was too far from the city. He wanted to raise his kids in a peaceful, natural environment.

After a long drive, the Mehtas finally reached the house after sunset. It was dark, and the kids, who had fallen asleep during the drive, didn't see much as they arrived. However, Mrs. Mehta was struck by the beauty of the surroundings. The only thing that bothered her was the isolation—there was no other house within 500 meters. Mrs. Mehta made porridge for the children and put them to bed. The next morning, the kids woke up feeling more rested than ever.

They rushed outside, eager to explore, and were mesmerized by what they saw. They weren't used to the sound of birds chirping or the gentle flow of a nearby stream. They saw rabbits playing in the grass, but when the kids approached, the rabbits scurried away. After a hearty breakfast, the Mehtas explored the large estate around their home. It felt like a holiday retreat, except this retreat was permanent.

Later that afternoon, they returned to the house. The wooden flooring was so cold that it was impossible to walk without slippers. The floors creaked, making footsteps audible even upstairs. The rooms were large, and the kids enjoyed running around. A few days passed, and one day, while the young boy was playing with his sister, he suddenly slipped on the floor. Just as he was about to crash into the wall, it felt as though something stopped him. He looked around but didn't see anyone—his sister was far behind. He thought perhaps he had regained his balance in time. His sister had a similar experience.

One day, during a strong wind, the kids were playing outside. The sister tried to open the door, but the wind pushed it shut. It was about to slam into her when it suddenly stopped mid-air and slowly closed. She was stunned. The children told their mother about these incidents, and while she was relieved they were safe, she reminded them to be careful.

A few days later, a new servant joined the household to help with chores. The servant was reclusive and rarely spoke to anyone, which initially bothered the Mehtas, but they soon ignored it. One day, the servant approached Mrs. Mehta when she was alone and asked why her family had chosen this house when there were nicer villas in the area.

Mrs. Mehta was irritated by the question and told the servant that she trusted her husband's decisions and was happy with their choice. However, the thought lingered in her mind, and she brought it up with her husband. Mr. Mehta explained that it was a great deal for the price and location. Still, his wife wondered why no one had lived in the house for 28 years. They decided to have the house checked for *Vaastu*, so they called a renowned priest from their hometown. To their surprise, the priest said the house had perfect *Vaastu*—it balanced prosperity and harmony. He even mentioned that if they ever faced danger outside, they would be safe inside the house, as it had a powerful aura. This explanation reassured Mrs. Mehta, who now believed the house was protecting the children during their near-misses.

Meanwhile, Mr. Mehta was getting to know his new neighbors. Most of the homes were seldom occupied, as they were used as holiday homes. One of his neighbors, Mr. Kannan, invited him over for tea. When Mr. Mehta arrived, he noticed that Mr. Kannan's house looked like a vintage structure, well-maintained and clearly lived in for a long time. During their conversation, Mr. Kannan asked if anything was troubling him. Mr. Mehta shared his concerns about the new house and the rumors he had heard. Mr. Kannan advised him not to pay attention to gossip, explaining that people had unjustly tarnished the reputation of the house. Curious, Mr. Mehta asked why anyone would do such a thing. Sensing Mr. Mehta's need for the full story, Mr. Kannan began recounting the history of the house.

Back then, it was known as Banerjee Villa, owned by a Bengali family, the Banerjees. Mr. Banerjee was a journalist for a renowned newspaper. Though people said the family held certain orthodox beliefs, Mr. Kannan's experience was different. The Banerjees kept to themselves, and their children often played in the garden. Despite their reclusiveness, Mr. Banerjee was close to Mr. Kannan's father, who was a retired editor. The two men would often discuss controversial topics, including the refugee movement in Kolkata, which Mr. Banerjee was writing about and receiving backlash for. Mr. Banerjee found solace in the house, which he described as soothing and relaxing. He often dreamed of a secret passage behind the kitchen courtyard but could never quite make sense of it. Then, one night, something terrible happened.

Miscreants, posing as holidaymakers, had been lurking in the area. They planted black magic dolls, bones, and pictures of local children around the Banerjee property. The next morning, the Banerjees found footprints around their estate and sensed they were being followed. Mr. Banerjee quickly packed up his family, intending to leave. But before they could, a mob gathered outside, shouting accusations of black magic.

Trapped, Mr. Banerjee tried to find the secret passage from his dream. Unfortunately, no one knows what happened next, but the family was found dead the next day under mysterious circumstances. The house was falsely rumored to be cursed and haunted by black magic. However, those close to the Banerjees knew this wasn't true.

After hearing the story, Mr. Mehta felt at peace. But one day, the Mehta family mysteriously disappeared without a trace. Mr. Kannan, concerned, visited the house and found it in disarray, as though someone had broken in. Later, he learned that Mr. Mehta was a fraud, having duped investors into a hedge fund scam. He had forged documents, changed his identity, and fled to this house. It wasn't long before his location was traced, but by the time the police arrived, Mr. Mehta had vanished. How he escaped remained a mystery. Perhaps the secret passage was real.

Reflecting on this, Mr. Kannan realized that the house behaved according to the character of its residents. It had grown so attached to the Banerjees that it didn't reveal the passage, as it didn't want them to leave. But when Mr. Mehta's deceit was uncovered, the house showed him the way out. Mr. Kannan likened this to the way people cling to bad memories, unable to let go. In the end, holding on too tightly can lead to regret.

10

THE SQUIRREL AND THE SAGE

Once upon a time, there was a tiny squirrel. It stayed on a pine tree in a forest. It used to hop from one tree to the other in search of nuts. It liked nuts so much that other animals in the forest used to call him Nutty. Nutty was very mischievous in nature and made a peculiar squeaking sound.

Whenever it crossed the paths of other animals, they would instantly identify his sound. Other animals used to be in awe of him, as his tummy was always full. Unlike other animals who were not able to satisfy their hunger every time, Nutty used to get what he wanted very easily.

One day a sage came to the forest and started staying in a hutment there. The sage had a cult following of devotees who started visiting the sage in his abode.

Gradually, he became very popular amongst the devotees. Whenever they would visit the sage, they would bring him nuts and fruits from the forest. The sage used to feast on the tasty fruits and nuts of the forest after his sermons.

Nutty was once very hungry in the morning and started exploring the usual trees from where he got his food. Unfortunately, that day none of the trees bore any fruits or nuts. This made Nutty very worried. It thought, how come all the nuts and fruits have disappeared suddenly? It was pondering when a bird came and sat on a branch. The bird saw the squirrel worried and asked what happened. Nutty said that he was unable to find any nuts or fruits and that he was very hungry.

The bird then told the squirrel that there was a sage who stayed nearby and it saw all his devotees come there in the morning and pluck nuts and fruits from all the nearby trees to give as an offering to the sage. This made the Nutty very angry. It went straight to the sage's hut and indeed saw that there were a lot of nuts and fruits there.

So, he went to the sage and said, "O wise man, why do you thrive on my food? If you would consume the fruits and nuts of the forest, then what will the other animals eat? You are a human being and are capable of eating grains and plants. But you avoid eating that and only eat nuts and seeds. If your devotees continue doing this, there will be nothing left in the forest for small animals like me."

This made the sage realise his mistake. He immediately summoned his followers and requested them to bring him grains and other food as an offering in the future. The wise old man thanked Nutty for opening his eyes and said he will never replenish from the resources of the forest that are meant for animals like him.

11

THE BLINDFOLD

Have you ever imagined something really positive coming out of a calamity? Someone who thinks this is just the right situation to start. Well, if you go nuts pondering over this thought, then you are in for a shocking surprise.

Pretend you are playing Blindfold. Your eyes are tied and friends are dodging you; you somehow get hold of someone's hand and pass on the turn to the other. For any other person, this game lasts only until you have the blindfold on. But for Rubin, the blindfold was always tied to him. Now we come to the real story.

A bright young boy, Rubin, was determined to reach the stars someday. He was an exceptionally bright kid, unlike other kids of his age. He had a different perspective on all things, and that was what differentiated him from the others. His parents loved him a lot, and they never stopped him from exploring different things.

They taught him to be independent right from an early age and to make the right use of time. He liked to be in his own company, and even though he was friendly, he was a bit introverted.

So he spent most of his time reading books, cycling, and also had an advanced science lab at his home curated by his father. Experiments were his favourite pastime. He used to make his own analyses and jot them down in his book. But not every day can be a rosy day.

On one busy Monday, while going for a science exploration event on his cycle, a car sped across the alley and lost control, eventually hitting him on his head. Passersby rushed him to the hospital and called up his parents. They came rushing to the hospital. Although there was a lot of bleeding, paramedics somehow managed to save his life. However, it was never the same again. Rubin lost his eyesight in both eyes. His hopes and dreams came crashing down. His parents could not accept his fate. They tried everything possible and went to the best hospitals to save his eyesight, but were unsuccessful. The nerves that supply oxygen to the eyes got ruptured in the accident, and even though his eyes suffered no damage as such, still his eyesight could not be restored. Paul and Molly, i.e., his parents, decided it was up to them to give Rubin the life he deserved.

Molly was a very practical lady and she started grooming Rubin. She did not want Rubin to always have a helping hand for anything and wanted him to be independent just like he was earlier. This would give him the much-needed confidence and he would not feel frustrated. Although Rubin's mental state at this point was weak, he still tried to cope up and started learning things that every blind person does. But he had to face a lot of struggle. Paul, who was seeing all this, was feeling helpless.

Unlike his better half, Paul was a little emotional and Rubin's condition was making him feel bad every passing day. Sometimes he felt it was just too much and maybe Rubin could not take in what Molly was trying to impart. But on the other hand, he wanted Rubin to be strong enough and knew this was the only way he could.

On the other hand, Molly was handling severe depression and was on medicines. One day she called up Paul by her bed and said no matter what happens to her, he should be strong and raise Rubin just like any normal kid. And then the unforeseen happened. Molly passed away and Paul went into a state of delirium. His son gave him strength at this moment. Paul realised there was no one else for Rubin except him and he had to be strong.

Several days passed. He saw that Rubin was withdrawing into a shell and losing his confidence because his mother was not with him. Paul then decided he would have to continue what Molly did for Rubin, but in a different way. Paul then found a way out. One morning, he called Rubin and said, 'Let's play Blindfold'. Rubin thought to himself that he was already blind and how could they play. Paul said he would put a blindfold on himself and asked Rubin to dodge him. It was fun at first for the father-son duo, but what Paul was trying to do was to experience how it feels to be blind and whether his mind can make out what his eyes cannot. Paul started doing things differently. This not only helped

Rubin navigate things better but also helped Paul train him to listen to sounds, smell, touch, and make better use of his other senses.

Gradually his other senses became stronger and Rubin started growing more confident. He began learning again and resumed his science lab experiments. His academic scores started improving and slowly he was on par with other kids.

Paul still wanted his kid to excel beyond what other kids could do, and he realised if his kid could reach the same level as others, he could easily surpass and reach beyond. On the other hand, Rubin established a deep bond with his father, his maturity level increased, he slowly started helping his father as he started getting old, and also realised his responsibilities at home. If there was one thing Paul could not give him, it was his eyesight. But there was something bigger he wanted to give his son. He remembered that every time he put on a blindfold, it helped him access deep layers of his mind to explore alternate realities. He wanted his son to get a little older, and now it was the right time.

He called up his son and said, "Your mind is more powerful than you could ever imagine. If you train it to see things, it will help you see. But if you train it to see beyond what the eyes can see, it will give you infinite possibilities and alternate realities."

Simply put, you can come out of a tragedy, or simply bounce back after a personal loss or even greater. Eventually, the impossible happened. Rubin learnt what no one could. To see the world through one's mind.

When he grew up, he became a scientific advisor to the core governing council. His team worked to create new possibilities in the world, mostly in terms of crisis.

During a plague outbreak, when the world came to a standstill and was held up in their homes, his team was working day in and day out studying seismic movements in the Earth's crust. This was to prevent another catastrophic calamity from occurring like major earthquakes. He felt this is an alternate reality that if not explored, can lead to further loss of lives.

His team was also significantly contributed to studying how varying landscapes over a period of time constitute the ecology of diseases from animals whose homes we have invaded over a period of time. In this world, you need such people too, as if you think along the same lines as others, Who would save the world? Let blindness not impair your mind. Let it open a plethora of possibilities, unimagined and fruitful.

'Wow, I really love this game- The Blindfold,' imagined Rubin, who was playing this game with his daughter Rose in his garden 20 years later.

12

THE SILENT TREMORS

I came across a geologist the other day. His name was Pritam. A geologist studies the Earth, the rocks of which they are composed, and how they change over time. When the continents were being formed due to shifting tectonic plates, a lot of study and research went into this subject. But over time, such studies lost steam, as no major geological changes were happening. Of course, the major distraction was Global warming and research shifted to that. Now Pritam used to join small research groups continuing to do what he was good at but the discoveries & results were not much discussed nor published anywhere. Due to this, many geologists started quitting & pursued other jobs for money.

Now Pritam was fond of photography. Who pays a geologist these days, he thought, and so he started exploring a parallel career in photography. In the current age, where it's all about social media & Instagram reels. He shot weddings, birthday events, baby arrival events, etc and started earning a decent amount of money.

However, what was missing was the thrill!

When he saw what his other batchmates were doing and they were much ahead in their career, he was very desperate to make it big. In the middle of all this, there was a conflict going on between Russia and Ukraine. Pritam had a friend in Ukraine and while talking to him on a call the other day, he gave the idea of war tourism. As Pritam was already in a frustrated state of mind, he somehow managed to get an air ticket to Ukraine and flew the next day. His friend was doing a project for the Army; so he arranged a couple of gate passes for himself and Pritam to visit the war-torn region.

When they visited the region, there were bodies of people lying around everywhere, some of them were wounded. Pritam started taking pictures of those people, as he wanted to sell it back in India. His friend Alok was a little surprised to see this and asked Pritam whether he was not deeply affected by the state of the people around him. To which Pritam said "No". He then asked him why was he taking pictures of such people, Pritam said there was a stream in photography called 'Conflict Photography' and he just wanted to produce his exhibits for a renowned conflict photographer Shyam Prasad Kerkar. His idea was to win his trust so that he could accompany him for his assignments. Alok lauded the idea and helped him take many more pictures. In the evening that day, he organized all the pictures in a separate folder on his laptop.

The next day he left for India. When he met Shyam and showed him his work, he was appreciated. Shyam promised to take him along for his next assignment.

Eventually, Pritam started assisting Shyam. He visited places that had famine, visited villages that were washed out in heavy rains, etc. His pictures captured the pain of people, it showed their helplessness. The emotions came out so vividly bright in his pictures, that they slowly started circulating in the national news and from then his journey took a turn for the better.

Pritam could have been happy with the mileage he was getting, but his greed to earn a name for himself in the international circles, made him take a step that one could not imagine.

One day while he was sitting back home thinking about what his life would have been if he were still a geologist, something struck in his mind. Why not dig deeper into the core of the earth and find out places in the world where there could be earthquakes? Japan was one such country that was reeling from lot of earthquakes and he thought that was the best opportunity. So one day he packed his bags and left for Japan. There he started analyzing the movements inside the surface and prepared a pattern when such earthquakes are most likely to occur. His analytical predictions slowly started coming true. Even before the earthquake would occur, he would reach the spot and camp his gear there. Photographs started streaming in real-time and the world was shocked. He started getting paychecks in millions.

With course of time, he collaborated with the media charging hefty fees. While he was basking in the success of glory he achieved out of all this, the Japanese, who are a lot more conservative, disciplined, mild-mannered

& hardly confrontational, were getting disturbed by news covering their country's calamities which showed them in poor light. Despite their dedication towards restoring houses and damaged properties with sheer hard work and determination, they did not like the attention they were getting from the world, as they were a reserved country. They wanted to fix matters before it escalated further.

Pritam was staying in a lodge in Okinawa which the Japanese Government came to know. One day, they evacuated the entire lodge and the area surrounding that place and planted IEDs around the streets, and small buildings which demolished the area and also detonated mines which were secretly buried underneath the ground, during World War 2. Later they propagated the news that there were mild tremors observed due to which some of the buildings collapsed. Pritam's death was reported as collateral damage. For the Japanese, it was not much of a resurrection. They built back the place in no time just like usual. But what started big for Pritam, ended on such a small note without the world knowing the true reality. It was a well-deserved lesson for him not to capitalize on the helplessness of another nation/ people.

Many people in his fraternity suspected and eventually realized that there was something fishy with the way his life ended, but for them too it was a lesson hard learned not to mess up with something for one's own benefit. From then on, ethical standards were practiced in conflict photography.

13

BACK-TRACK

Someone once asked me, "What does it take to rewind old memories?" Most of the time, we love to recollect the happy ones. Sometimes, you feel as if you could relive those moments. But has the thought ever crossed your mind if you could alter them, especially the ones that you don't want to remember, or at least change the outcome of those moments? Would it not add to another happy memory?

Back then, I was working on a new secret military project related to a time-shift approach. It was primarily designed to change the outcome of an event that had catastrophic consequences. We were part of a team of physicists, and our first experiment with time shift emerged successful. It was an amazing moment for us all. We had delved into the mind of a psychotic suicide bomber who was about to carry out a terrorist bombing on a large scale, played with his neurons in simple language, if I would say, and manipulated his thoughts. This not only helped us change the outcome but also made him reveal the mastermind behind the same.

It was a joyful moment for me, and I wanted to celebrate this success. As this was a covert operation and everyone involved had to disengage and isolate themselves for a few days as per standard protocol, we all went to our respective homes. As a token of appreciation for my efforts in leading the team, I was gifted an instance of this time-shift module, and then began my actual research.

When I came back home, my father, who is very close to me, was rejoiced on hearing my success story.

I was meeting him after quite a while, and we started discussing a lot of things. We wandered in the park on the weekend, that is when he recited something about his old days to me. He said he always felt incomplete in life as most of the choices he made were wrong.

Despite being a kind-hearted and happy-go-lucky guy then, he just took everything in his stride and progressed in life. His marriage to my mom was not the best choice either, which I was also aware of. Though his courtship lasted for quite a long time, the reason for the bond to stay alive, I realised only later, which was me. All those times I sensed he was always looking for something to motivate him.

My dad was a bundle of talent, and I knew whatever he stepped into, he would eventually do it with dedication and heart. But then that day in the park, he accidentally revealed to me, although I didn't expect him to say anything like that to me at first, as he was introverted in nature. He told me about different phases of his life and the regret he had for his choices. He also told me about a secret crush he had on someone. It was something very nice to hear from him.

I always used to ask him, "What took you so long to move on in life and why did you compromise so much for my sake?" Did he want me to have a normal, happy childhood with mum and dad? Did he not want my friends to make fun of me if he had just parted ways with my mother and left me? Or simply because his love for me was greater than any of his needs. He didn't have an answer. He just shook his head and said he was not sure. I also asked him if he tried to search for the person he had a crush on, and he said he never gave it a thought. Then after a certain period of time, he wanted to engage in humanitarian work, which he was very fond of. However, he could not do that as well, and when I asked him why, he just said he hated staying away from me. So I asked him, "How do you feel now when I am not with you all the time?" He said he had no choice. Our talks went on, and that day I realised how caring and compassionate he was towards everyone in his life, except himself.

We came back home after our stroll, and he went to his room to read a book. Something pondered in my mind. What if I could change at least 1 event in his life that could make him a different and happier person today? I knew I could not change his life forever, but at least it was worth an attempt.

So I took out my time-shift jukebox, decoded, and got exactly to that one specific moment of his life where he was sitting in a park waiting for the crucial thought to trigger his mind. While he was sitting there, his lady crush came out of nowhere and sat beside him. She confessed she too had a crush on him and asked him not to worry too much about her. She told him maybe life has set different paths for both of them and they would not be together but should always hope one day they will meet again and in that hope remain happy. My dad was overwhelmed to see this moment that he could not hide his tears. All the love he buried underneath his heart suddenly flourished out and they gave each other a beautiful hug. Walking hand in hand, they strolled the park as if they would never meet again.

In that moment, there was deep unconditional love. I realised that was what my father was looking for all his life. Later when she was about to leave, she told him to pursue his passion of serving humanity for the better causes. She asked him not to worry about his daughter and also to start loving oneself first, so that no negative emotions run in his mind. Having said that, she bid farewell to him and left. My father became involved in various social activities of serving the needy, helping the underprivileged, started a fund for opening a hospital, and many more things. Eventually, he became the person he is today and he also spent his precious time with me. With the help of the time-shift jukebox, I unlocked his long buried secret which helped him be a better person. Unfortunately, stitched events of time cannot be recollected, but those moments have already given you beautiful memories and I keep reminding him of the old days.

You would be surprised how I could stitch this event back in time when I was still small then. Surprisingly, nothing changed for me. I only changed the outcome of the thought that germinated in his mind. In these busy times, it is not practically possible to get someone to be with you all the time, and you need to forge a bond with oneself. That bond is the best bond that we need to cherish in our life forever!

14

THE LITMUS TEST

Some of the most memorable days of life were those that we spent with our friends in college. Each day we would start from home early in the morning. We would reach college right on time but not with the intention of sitting for the first lecture. Rather, we would head straight to the gymnasium and fret our day out playing table tennis, badminton and carrom. We were champions in all facets of the game.

Later on during the break, we would spend our time chatting in the cafeteria to show our presence in college. The conversation ranged from the latest gizmos to some of the fastest bikes and cars. During weekends, we would take time off to some far-fledged area in the outskirts of the city where we would booze and eventually make fun of each other. In short, life was fun-loving and adventurous.

But then everyone desires a change in life. And then one fine day, we decided to sit for our first lecture, Chemistry. Despite knowing the antics of our group, our chemistry professor Ram Mohan Sharma used to be calm and extremely tolerant towards us. So we had immense regard and respect for him.

As I sat listening to his session, my eyes wandered around the class, in search of Pranaya. She was a short girl with a wheatish complexion. We were classmates right since school days. I used to take notes from her just before the exams since I never sat for lectures. Though she knew my reputation in college, she was always kind to me, and that made me garner a soft corner for her in my heart.

Today I thought it was my turn to return a favour. I was jotting down the notes dictated by our professor and thought of lending them to her the next day. As planned, when I saw her entering the classroom the forthcoming day, I started towards her and said, "Here's what you missed yesterday." Just then I heard someone saying, "Hey, what a big joke, a person who never sat for lectures all through the academic year is trying to share his notes." I felt disappointed, but then Pranaya consoled me saying, "Don't mind, dear, you cannot stop tails from wagging." It was then that I realised how much faith she had in me. This moment was a defining moment in my life. I started attending lectures regularly and started improving my scores. During chemistry practicals, I always used to be with Pranaya trying to help her out, as she was a bit scared of chemicals.

My friends started realising that I was trying to ignore them. One fine day they said, "It's good to see you take life seriously, but never forget us and whenever you need us, just let us know." I was shocked on hearing this and realised that they were my best pals and how well they understood me. It was this kind gesture that forced me to reveal to them about my feelings for Pranaya. Though they pulled my legs at first, but eventually they encouraged me. I was waiting for the right moment to express my feelings to her.

It was just before the preliminary exams of HSC, when I gathered tremendous courage to tell her what I thought about her. Pranaya was shocked to hear this and said that she preferred to spend her life with a successful person, not with a person who does not have an ambition in life. On hearing this, I felt devastated.

I decided to teach her a lesson on the day of our final practical exams. I was standing at the corner near the door just waiting for her to complete her test and emerge out. The lab assistant was busy collecting the test papers and our supervisor along with the external examiner had already left. When she was through with her test and submission of her paper, she started towards the door, unaware that I was standing just near the door with my back facing her. I started to follow her, with a beaker filled with concentrated sulphuric acid in hand. In a fit of rage, I stretched my hands to splash acid on her face from behind. Just then, our chemistry professor Ram Mohan Sharma came out from the neighbouring class, where he was a supervisor, and then held me back and asked me what I was doing. I told him not to stop me. By then, Pranaya had already reached the stairs but fortunately did not spot me in this situation. "Son, I can understand your feelings," said the professor trying to gauge the situation. By now, he was well aware of what prompted me to this juncture. "But let me just give you a small example on a test that you all perform in the lab. It's called the Litmus test which states that "Acids turn neutral litmus paper red and bases turn it blue". If you visualise yourself to be in the position of the litmus paper and suppose that a person has entered your life, it is you who decide the nature of the influence the person has on you. If you interpret what Pranaya said to you in a negative sense, then you end up judging her influence as something bad (acidic), whereas if you take her words seriously in a positive manner, you may well end up taking up the challenge of proving your worth." This moment was a defining moment in my life.

Today, after 15 years, I was attending the Nobel Laureates Conference held in Madrid. I was nominated this year along with Alex Romanov from Russia for our joint efforts in the field of nanotechnology. During the press conference, I was searching for someone. As I saw Prof Ram Mohan Sharma making himself comfortable in the guest row, I was convinced. But when I took my eyes off that place, I sensed that I missed something, and then I glanced back.

Pranaya was also there with Prof Sharma. Maybe he thought that the person who changed my life should also be present on this honourable day. After the function, I went down to see Prof Sharma to seek his blessings. But I ignored Pranaya. On seeing this, Prof Sharma introduced me to her, "Meet my daughter Pranaya." I was left spellbound by his words.

Today, we all worship those heroes who rose from the ashes and reached for the sky. In life, there is always a turning point. Maybe you will give credit to the girl who gave me an opportunity to show that I can take up a challenge and emerge successful in life. But then are we forgetting someone else too? It takes ordinary people like us to show what we are capable of. But it takes extraordinary people like Prof. Sharma to prove it is extremely difficult to balance the roles that you play in life. He is the real hero because he was in extreme pain to see that his daughter was in grave danger when I was about to pour acid onto her. Just imagine the plight of a father who would have been a witness to this incident.

Despite this, instead of handing me over to the police, he just gave a simple, but powerful example, which changed my life forever. Thus he not only protected his daughter by playing a father's role but also accelerated me to this position, in a mentor's role. So let us salute our teachers who took great pain in making us believe what we are capable of.

15

BEYOND THE GRAVE

The only good thing about this moment is that it will pass. With this hope, we lead our lives. Someone might lose an opportunity, whether it's a milestone to achieve for a professional in their daily work or not getting selected for an interview as a newcomer. But once the day goes and the next day comes, our lives are recharged; we start chasing our dreams again and finish off unfulfilled tasks.

For someone who is in pain today, the thought—or simply the possibility—that it will be gone is enough to cheer for. The mental state of an individual does not last long; it shifts from sorrow to happiness, from fear to courage, from love to hate. The best advice we receive if we remain in a state for too long is to "Be Practical." But remember, all this holds true only if you are transitioning to an opposite physical or mental state.

With years of agony, pain, and lost hope, people need something else, and that's what this technology was built for. We are talking about Slumbera—an enhanced Generative AI-based Augmented Virtual Reality Model designed to give the less privileged another chance to be happy and pain-free. This was primarily modeled for cancer patients, who endure irreparable damage to their cells and bodies, resulting in immense pain and discomfort. It creates a virtual space that enables them to transition seamlessly from a crippled state to a coma-like sleep state, where they actually live in an alternate reality filled with joy and happiness, albeit temporarily, to escape their pain. What a life it would be for them! Nirvana Tech, the pioneer behind this life-changing technology, had just received funding from the top three medical giants for this research.

The pilot cancer project was a success right away. A video presentation was prepared and shown to the regulatory, judiciary, and parliamentary committee. Impressed by the results, the act was passed to approve this technology. Slumbera finally launched on December 18, 2029. I volunteered for the test in excitement, being part of the research team during the launch, and what I saw and felt was remarkable and unbelievable. It was a different world of infinite possibilities; the themes were customized based on your genetic and cultural history, making them unique for each participant in the program. The only hiccup was the cost factor. There was pressure to subsidize the cost and make it affordable for many people.

Slowly, the medical fraternity expanded its reach, and Slumbera became a subscriber-based open-source household model where anyone could subscribe. There were different packages offered, from a slumber of two hours to a slumber of ten days, and some that spanned a few months. At first, there was a lot of opposition to the decision to roll this out to the masses, as the entire objective was to eradicate the persistent state of pain or suffering in vulnerable people. However, once the popularity increased, demand skyrocketed. Over time, this became a common man's tool.

Many years passed...

Today is August 21, 2179. The world is much happier than before. Everyone is lost in their own unique world of Slumbera. It is indeed the Slumber Era. Everyone had to grapple with the wounds that World War III inflicted. The grief of personal loss had to be eased, the pain of suffering had to diminish, and the hurt of wounds had to fade away. People had to cope with job loss, depression, poverty, hunger, and countless other issues posed by this deadly war. This temporary state of happiness was their best refuge.

Who would have guessed that this state-of-the-art medical marvel would become the lifeline of humanity? Who knows whether people would take this with them beyond the grave!

16

TOTALITY

Not so long back, there were 2 best friends, Srushti and Gyaan. They grew up together, played together, danced and sang in the rain. They lived in a large jungle surrounded by vast oceans. Srushti was happy in this small world of hers, but Gyaan always wanted to explore beyond the oceans. He told Srushti about his wish and they decided to explore.

One day, Gyaan found a huge log of wood from a heap and made a boat to float. They started in the morning but by evening, they were still in the middle of the sea. Suddenly there was a storm and their boat capsized. However, both of them knew how to swim even in rough waters and somehow managed to find a small island.

When they reached there, they were very tired. On this island, there lived a sorcerer. He saw them both and invited them over to his house. He was evil in nature. He fed them good food and they stayed over at his house overnight. In the morning, when they were about to leave the place, he called them over and said there was a magnificent cave located nearby which they should see before leaving. Both of them agreed.

When they reached the cave, the sorcerer told them that there was a crystal ball, which would show them their future. Gyaan was very excited but Srishti was reluctant at first, however, she agreed later. The only condition was they could not gaze at the crystal ball together. Each would get their own chance.

The crystal ball indeed showed them the future world. But each of them had different views. One showed the vast expanse of oceans and seas filled with aquatic life, snow-capped peaks of mountains and every other wonderful creation of nature that Srusti had not witnessed in her life. She actually wanted to witness them. In her mind, there were always doubts and so she went through all that the crystal ball had to show. What she saw in the end baffled her as none of the beautiful creations of nature showed up in the end.

On the other hand, Gyaan always wanted to see Srushti happy and fulfil all her wishes. He saw in the crystal maze whatever good was about to happen and make life easier for her. It showed him that age-old *chulhas* would be replaced by automatic gas, old wells used to bore water would be replaced by storage tanks, and beautiful ornaments made out of rare minerals that would look good on her. He also saw numerous opportunities for everyone to work and mankind would not be confined to just hunting and agriculture.

In the interim, he missed seeing minute details in between. He also ended up watching mid-way and concluded that the future was indeed good. The sorcerer was clever. He did not force Gyaan to watch till the end. Gyaan was excited to tell what he saw to Srushti. But Srushti was shocked to divulge to Gyaan what she saw.

When Gyaan came down the cave, whatever he saw in the future had already occurred. Gyaan was surprised to find tall buildings around, automatic cars, robotic machines, nuclear weapons, and diseases faced by mankind he never saw. He started searching for Srushti. But Srishti was gone. All nature that was around earlier was destroyed to build man-made structures. A lot of things had changed.

Gyann and Srushti denote Science and Nature. Science was intended to harness natural resources for the betterment of nature, including mankind. It wanted to give nature the best it could to preserve it and not allow it to fall prey to mankind.

The world embraced Gyaan for having shown them the path of science and innovation. But Gyaan failed in his actual purpose. He did not see what mankind would do for its selfish purpose of growth and greed. Srushti was scattered and all flora and fauna in the world got depleted.

Animal life was exploited to gain access to their skin, horns, tusks, and flesh, which had huge value in the market. Medical science had no doubt progressed, but mankind was harsh and started implanting harmful viruses in the human body to experiment. Whatever is left behind now is also in danger.

We, as responsible human beings, should come forward to preserve and extend nature by taking all possible steps so that our future generations remember the true bond between Science and Nature.

17

THE GOLDEN HARVEST

Roselyn was a lovely, sweet little girl who enjoyed playing with butterflies. She had a wonderful family consisting of a doting father, a caring mother, and a loving elder sister. Though she was a down-to-earth girl, she was more attached to the countryside. While other children of her age liked to play with toys like dolls and kitchen sets, she used to play with sand and seeds. One day her grandfather took her to the far-off contours of the countryside, where she got to explore forests and streams. It was a lovely experience for her.

While returning, she had a strange experience and felt like going there every day. As she grew up, her friends started bullying her. They noticed she was more engrossed in playing with natural things like bubbles, sand, water, etc. She became an introvert as she didn't have many friends. It was not that she was unfriendly, just that her fascinations were a little different from the others. They told her to go and stay in a cave, as that is where she belonged.

Any other girl would wish to stay in a dream castle, but she was someone who liked challenges and was very determined. So she thought that one day she would indeed go and stay in a cave. She expressed this desire to her family. Her mother did not like this idea and straightaway said no. However, her father and sister were understanding enough. They knew she was a fearless girl and even if they said no, she would find some means to go there. Her father had a friend who was a hunter. His family was very close to theirs. He called him up and explained the situation. The hunter friend convinced her father to leave her with them one day and he would manage the situation.

So one fine day, she packed her bags and left for the jungle. The hunter uncle and his family welcomed her to their house. She had researched about the place she was planning to go and kept ample supplies with her for the trip. She was accompanied by the hunter uncle. They went there a little early to ward off unwanted visitors like bats and snakes which could reside inside. The hunter uncle set up a tent with a campfire lit for the night. Roselyn stayed in the cave that night and lived her dream.

At sunrise, her uncle asked her how the experience was. She was delighted and said she had the best sleep of her life. She also said she had a feeling she belonged to this place. In the morning, the chirping sound of birds and rustling sound of trees made the atmosphere even more splendid. She went to the stream and played there for a while. On the way back from the stream, she sat beneath a large oak tree. When her uncle came to search for her, he saw the girl sitting beside a tree as if talking to someone. But when he reached there, he only saw the girl. He asked her with whom she was talking to. But she said there was no one to talk to there. Her hunter uncle felt a bit strange.

They left the place after a hearty lunch. On coming back home, she was so filled with joy and shared all her experiences with her family. They were happy for her. When it was evening, she went to the park and narrated the cave experience to the girls who bullied her before. Then she went to a corner and sat there and started mumbling as if she was speaking to someone. The girls playing there got anxious as Roslyn didn't have any friends. They were surprised to find she was indeed speaking to someone not visible to them. They got a little scared at first.

One of the girls said, "Let's tell this to everyone." News spread far and wide that Roslyn was out of her mind, speaking to herself all the time. Her uncle also narrated the experience he saw in the jungle. Her parents got a little worried. However, the truth was that Roselyn had created an imaginary friend in her mind and liked talking to her. But people around her thought she was not mentally stable and started poking fun at her. This irked her more.

At first, she didn't have many friends and now whoever she saw was only making fun of her. That is when she decided she would go back to the jungle. That day after school, she didn't get off at her home from the bus. She got off at the last stop and from there headed to the jungle. She went straight to the oak tree. Suddenly a voice came, "What brings you here today?" Roslyn said she was tired of this world. She said no one bothered to understand her. The voice once again came, "You have us. Then why do you need this world to understand you? We are your friends."

Roslyn had forged a deep bond with the jungle, so deep that she could whisper and talk to all the trees. They were her closest friends. Seeing her in agony, they asked her if there was any way by which they could help. As Roselyn was filled with anger, she demanded something from the trees that was not in the true spirit. She wanted them to stop giving life-saving oxygen to the people for 1 day. The trees were shocked to hear this from Roselyn. They told her they do not exhale oxygen into the environment in return for something. They are selfless beings who only love to garner unconditional love and support for other living beings. Their mere existence was to give life to the other living beings. Even if God were to come down on Earth and ask for this, they would never bow to this request. The trees said 'We are not the supreme living beings bestowed with intelligence. Instead, we are the humble ones who give shelter to someone from the Sun and rain. Our entire purpose in life is to make use of every part of our body, be it root, stem, fruits, flowers, or leaves in some way for all other living beings. So if you were to ask us to stop giving oxygen to the others, we would never oblige'.

After that day, Roselyn knew the true difference between humans and trees. She was never able to communicate with the trees again. She was a gifted girl and the trees knew that. They had seen her future and that is how they had forged a deep bond with her. When she grew up, she became a crusader for saving the green cover. Her continued efforts and hard work changed the perspective of millions of others who also lent their support to her and not only became her true friends but also her followers.

Even today, while she is on her expedition to any jungle, she feels goosebumps, as if someone is trying to communicate with her. They wave at her when she comes to them; these signals only Roselyn knows. She knows that whatever she is today is only because of them and owes her life to them. She laughs at the silly thoughts that came to her when she was a child but also feels proud to have done something for these evergreen life-saving beings. She tells everyone to plant more trees and has written her book today 'The Golden Harvest'

18

ENGULF

I was sitting in a psychiatrist's clinic gazing at a painting on the wall. I was called in for my turn. There was a case file that I had already filled up that had reached her desk. The psychiatrist went through the case file, nodded her head, and said, 'Interesting'. "So you are scared of heights."

A couple of years later, I was an investigative journalist. Something interesting had come to me, something no one had dared to get into. It was a dark mystery about random children disappearing without leaving any trace. The police authorities were summoned, but none of the law enforcement officials expressed much interest. I found it astonishing to hear a couple of them who had gathered quite a few details about the case quit midway and they also refused to share any details about the case. Some mysteries simply do not have any answers and are better kept buried. They are weird to believe too. This was one of those. It was a difficult thing to crack with lots of homework to do. As there was no info shared, I had to start from scratch. I started with collecting records of victims who disappeared.

The mysterious disappearance of kids around the world cannot be just a coincidence. It has to have some meaning or connection. When I lay my hands on this long unsolved mystery that no one bothered to delve into much, I knew I was getting into dark territory.

My investigation started with finding commonalities between missing people. They could be related to anything like the same school, the same locality, people who could have some grudge against the victims, or even as simple as settling old scores with the victims or their families. I tried to narrow down to the minutest detail but didn't find any common factor to influence my investigation. Then I traced their habits, places where they would go and people they would meet. I searched their homes, their school bags, and their books. I went through their parents' phones, data, pictures, etc. Asked them to share their experiences. They were not even sure if their kids were still alive. Three months passed, and I knew my investigation was not headed in any direction.

My old classmate Drishti was into Analytics then and she suggested a brilliant idea. She told me the person/group responsible for the disappearance of kids could be looking out for common traits and that is where analytics could help. I shared the victims' data with her. She checked the Govt database and then tried to trace contacts associated with them. Most of them didn't cooperate much as the cases were pretty old. Our basic agenda was to identify the victims' SWOTs (Strengths, Weaknesses, Opportunities, Threats). Strengths were many but not quite significant as per the contacts. We tried to get into Opportunities and Threats together as there was a close link between them in terms of crime. That didn't help us much too. The last thing left was their weakness. They were significant as each of the contacts could remember the victims' weaknesses and fears closely.

One of the boys was afraid of spiders, one had claustrophobia, and one girl had concussion on seeing blood. There were many more. We kept this finding aside. Their search notices were issued throughout the world. This was to check trafficking of children rampant in some parts of the world. But not even one positive response was received. This was something strange. Either they have been wiped off from the world without leaving any trace. This was, however, too difficult to digest as at least their bodies should have been found. This was the worst I could imagine but I seriously wanted the kids to be alive. There was one possibility everyone was discussing. This was either they all were taken to a common place and before any rescue operations could reach them, there is a possibility that some accident occurred leading to the mysterious death of everyone who was abducted. But this was just another assumption. Without any concrete evidence, things got difficult to prove.

Days passed and my mind slowed down. I knew I needed a break. So the next day the first thing in the morning I left for an excursion with my ex-colleagues from the office. It was a welcome change. Got to engage in different activities and had lots of fun. After spending 2 days relaxing, I knew I had to get back to my unfinished assignment. I started for the office. On the way, I was going through The Herald. An interesting article caught my attention. The article was about how history repeats itself after a certain period. Back in the 1920s, there was a flu epidemic that took a lot of innocent lives and now after 100 years came another one on similar lines which everyone was fighting.

My intuition led me to believe this disappearance of children was also a pattern, and I set forth to check the previous incidents. I was startled to find out that exactly a century back, similar such incidents were reported which also went unsolved. I went almost 3 centuries back; it was difficult to collect the old data at first but somehow was able to trace similar incidents of multiple kids being abducted in a specific period, and my doubts came true. Now my task was simple: to find out what started this cataclysmic event which was neither a planned abduction nor any accident. Whatever I was investigating now was more out of curiosity. I was getting closer and closer to something but was skeptical; this was getting beyond what scientific explanation had to offer, and I was not sure if the world would accept or believe this.

My investigation ended with the famous hospital fire of South Harlington. The reason it ended here is the chain of events started shortly after the deadly fire that broke out. They call it the devil's carnage. The intensity of the fire was so severe that around 350 children and 73 adults were dead. The fire caught up at a vaccination camp and that day a lot of small kids were assembled there.

In that sudden fire that erupted, innocent children were charred to death. Even today the locals recall what their older generations told them about that fire. The children screamed in pain, many of them had severe burns while the others got suffocated to death. The screams echoed in the entire village and the fire tore apart the souls of the villagers. Post that incident many local people left the town, as if it was a jinxed place. It was left abandoned. No proper burial or last rites were done after the deadly accident. When I reached there, that place had an eerie sense of calm that you cannot witness anywhere.

As I strolled the old hospital site, I came across a piece of note, it was torn and the ink had faded. From what was left I could make out 'If you unravel the mystery, it takes its form.' I kept that in my shirt pocket and left the site without any clue. Also, I had collected photos of the children from old records. Many of those faces got etched in my mind. Now my task was to correlate to the current scenario. I tried to match the count of hospital victims with the missing kids. In the first occurrence of disappearance, the same number of kids went missing. In the second occurrence, the count doubled. My doubts and fears came to rest. I knew this phenomenon was growing exponentially. I came back home and wondered what this could be. I recorded all my findings in a file and uploaded the same. This looked to me like something supernatural. I was damn tired.

As I lay on the couch listening to music to soothe my nerves, I fell asleep. Even in my deep sleep, I could sense the cries of the children and their pain. I was in deep sorrow. Suddenly, I was awakened by a knock on the door. I was not expecting anyone so late. Hesitantly,

I opened the front door. Not seeing anyone, I tried to step my foot outside. That is when I realised there was no ground beneath my feet, as if I was perched at the top of a cliff and had nothing below. At first, I thought it was a dream. Then, when I realised it was indeed real, I got extremely scared and tried to rush back inside. Upon coming inside, I saw a smog-like form in front of me. I cleared my eyes, as if my vision was distorted. Even after clearing them, I could still see the smoggy form. It swayed a little at first, then stood intact. Inside the form, I could see events of the past - the hospital fire and the faces of those innocent children crying in pain who were killed. There were many small hands trying to come out of that form, hands of the kids who were trapped in the fire, as if they were trying to escape. On the verge of escaping, they would pull others inside the form, these were those kids who went missing later. This went on as if it was a chain reaction. It was a dreadful sight. The collective fears of all the children kept making the form stronger.

I sensed the children who died in the fire wanted to fulfil their dreams that were shattered in the fire. They saw these same dreams in the minds of other children from the later generations. So that is what related to the story of the missing children in the next 2 centuries too. Strangely, the missing children had the same characteristics as those who died in the fire. This form used their weaknesses and fears, to hypnotise them and pull them inside it. I coined this form The Engulf, as it engulfed the lives of those who it considered were more fortunate than the innocent kids who died in search of fulfilling their unfulfilled dreams.

Have you ever imagined coming face to face with the worst fears of your life with nothing else besides you to hold on to, and then going into a state of trance before being absorbed by an invisible force? This form is first born in our mind in the form of our fears, and it manifests itself slowly before gulping you. But sadly, this story is more like a fairy tale than reality.

I was always afraid of heights right since childhood, and that is why I had approached the psychiatrist earlier. 'If you unravel the mystery the Engulf takes form' is what the note in my pocket conveyed earlier, but I didn't take it seriously then. But when the ground vanished from beneath me, making me feel like I was left hanging, defying gravity with nothing below, I knew I was coming face to face with my worst fear of life, the fear of heights. After this, the Engulf took its form!

I wish I had more time to convey this to the world, but I don't think that would help much, as if they would believe me. I wish all the forthcoming generations to lead a happy, fearless life.

19

THE FRIENDLY GIANT

Once upon a time, there stayed a Giant in a jungle. Unlike what we would presume him to be, he was otherwise. He was friendly to the animals, did not hunt them, and thrived on plant foods. So the animals didn't feel any threat around him. The only thing that animals feared is this Giant would just jump out of nowhere to scare them and would then laugh aloud. His laugh echoed in the jungles, and the other animals would pause for a sec but later move on knowing that the Giant has succeeded in his plans for the day. The Giant derived great pleasure in doing this act and the targeted animal would curse the giant for this every time. Many of the animals apprehended the giant for this act and pleaded with him to stop this. But the Giant would just say that everyone needs a pastime and this was just one of his favourite pastimes. However, the Giant was humble at heart and always helped in times of need.

Every day a sage passed by the bylanes of the jungle where the giant used to stay. The giant never troubled the noble sage as it feared that the sage would curse him and that curse could come true. The sage knew the giant and he always stood by, speaking to the giant for a few minutes before proceeding ahead. The sage also made him realise that he was the protector of the jungle and should not abuse his authority and position. As the sage rightly said, the giant would protect the weaker animals from the stronger ones and helped in maintaining a balance in the jungle. He would stand for those in need.

After a few years, when the giant got a little old, he stayed aloof and did not bother the animals around. They wondered if something was wrong with him and went and told this to the sage. The next day the sage came to visit the giant and asked him why he remained so quiet these days and did not jump and laugh around scaring the other animals. On hearing this, the Giant said that he started getting worried that he was getting old and would die soon. So he stopped troubling the poor creatures.

The sage asked the giant if he would grant the giant another life after he died, whether he would be happy. The giant jumped with joy when he heard this. The sage told him that his spirit would stay alive inside the tallest tree of the jungle and he would not have any human form like he has today.

But this wish could only be fulfilled under one condition. In the years to come, when humans would evolve and procreate, they would expand beyond their boundaries and try to destroy these jungles to build their homes. If such a thing happens, then the Giant should scare them off from here just like he scared the animals.

The Giant said he was willing to do that, as the jungle was his home too, and then the sage muttered a secret prayer and made the giant immortal. The Giant became cheerful again. His friends, which are animals and birds, also became happy on seeing this. He wandered around the jungle freely and guarded it with grit and determination. Many more years passed.

One day he was gone, but his spirit stayed intact inside the tallest tree as the sage had said, and his laughter echoed around the jungle. Whenever any humans with evil intentions came inside the jungle with any evil intentions, he would scare them away. His tale was never forgotten. To the outside world, this jungle was haunted by the giant and no one would dare to venture inside and disturb its peace. While to the inside world of the jungle, the Giant's presence was still felt and this made them feel safe & secure instead. To this day, he never lets anyone with evil intentions venture inside the jungle.

20

THE FINAL LAP

Osborne was crawling on the ground with a push-along toy, when all of a sudden he lost control of it. Seeing the toy car race ahead, he rose up and took a few steps forward to get hold of it. "Thud!" As he plonked back on his bum, he started crying. His mom came rushing out of the kitchen. On seeing her baby crying, she went near him and said, "Come on, Os! Let's get up slowly and spring back to action."

As these words struck his mind, Osborne slowly gathered the wits to rise up. The only difference being, this time, he was a few hundred miles away from home in a vast stretch of forest. He was still trying to figure out the reason for his presence over there. He did not seem to remember anything. But he knew that he had to be there for a reason. His arms were tattered, and his head bore deep bruises, which were testimony to the fact that he had fallen from an elevated position.

Maybe due to this head injury, he had suffered a temporary memory lapse. So he could not recount his memories of late. Out of mere anxiety to escape, he started to introspect the surroundings. There were tall trees all around him. Mosses crawled to cover the long fallen trunks, each trunk tall and straight, many with bare branches below, only distinguishable from each other by the textures of their bark, or shape of their broadly reaching roots. These trunks were so large that they shielded the light coming from the sun. Though he did not know the exact time of the day, he could sense from the length of his shadow that it was afternoon. He could hear screeching sounds of wild animals echoing around the jungle. He had never heard such sounds before.

After walking a few yards, he started to feel dizzy. He realised that he did not have enough stamina to carry on. He then decided to take shelter beneath a tree. As he went near the tree, he heard a rattling sound. Just then he saw a wild rattlesnake emerging from a hole buried at the bottom of the tree with a big bandicoot in its mouth. The predator had captured its prey right at the bottom of the ground where it was holed up. It was clearly evident that there was no safe place in the jungle. Survival of the fittest was the protocol of the jungle. The philosophy was not much different at the racetrack too.

Well, it started a few years back when Osborne took part for the first time in a 200-meter race at his school sports meet. Surprisingly, he won that race. He started to participate in all the athletic events, and his tryst with destiny continued to prosper. Hopes transformed into ambition for this young lad. His hunger for winning became insatiable. Osborne's father used to encourage him in all these extracurricular activities. He himself was a sportsman in his early days.

He was now working as a civil engineer with a reputed construction firm. Osborne always shared a very close bond with his father, right since his childhood days. His father had gifted him the latest pair of sports shoes on his 12th birthday. Those shoes were specifically designed for athletics. Despite a hectic schedule, his father used to accompany him to all the sports events. It was a picture-perfect life for Osborne when suddenly everything took a topsy-turvy turn. One day his father was at a construction site when a slab fell on his head, damaging his skull. He succumbed to his injury even before he was admitted to the hospital. His mother took quite a few days to come out of this shock. Dire circumstances forced Osborne to take a part-time job as a delivery agent for a courier firm. He worked there in the evening after his classes.

During this period, his passion for the sport was slowly wearing off. Though his mother kept on pestering him to continue his interest in the sport, he simply ignored her pleas. His priorities in life had changed. There were more responsibilities on him now.

It was during his final year at school that the Red Cross Society organised a marathon event in his town. This was the moment his mother had been waiting for. She knew it was her son's summer holidays. He would not have any reason to avoid this event now. She managed to convince her son to participate. At first, he hesitated, though he reluctantly agreed. He was going to take part in an athletic event after 3 long years. Though he was less confident now, due to lack of practice, he still thought of giving it a try. He knew it was not going to be easy, as there might be stiff competition from unexpected quarters, and he was right. There was a guy by the name of Malcolm. He was from Royal Scottish school, a few miles away from Osborne's school, St. Peter's. Malcolm was a renowned athlete. He had claimed two successive championship titles in the preceding years. This time he was aiming to clinch his third, making it 3 in a row. Osborne knew it was not easy getting past Malcolm in the race. He was the favourite of the masses too. Osborne's spirits, though, were undeterred. As usual, he always loved challenges. There were banners all around the city. Spectators had flocked from all corners of the town to view this event.

Just a few minutes past 08:15 AM, the race started. There were drinks stalls at every 200 meters for the participant athletes to invigorate. En route, there were medical vans to monitor the physical status of the athletes. Private vehicles were restricted to ply on the streets that day.

After an hour of running, the position of the athletes was recorded. Malcolm was leading the race after 52 laps; there were still 3 laps to go. Osborne was not far behind; he was crossing his 50th lap. When the final lap began, Malcolm was just 200 meters ahead of Osborne. Osborne kept his nerves and gathered all the energy he could to accelerate his speed. He was on par with Malcolm, 50 meters from the finishing line. They were in sync for almost 8 seconds, after which Osborne slowly went past Malcolm and took the lead. The race was drawing to a close finish, and Osborne finally crossed the finishing line just 50 ms before Malcolm. Osborne had never contemplated that he would win. He gracefully hugged Malcolm after the event. But Malcolm gave a cold response, which he simply ignored. He was extremely happy. Osborne waved at his mom, who was sitting a few yards away. Osborne had made a successful comeback after disappearing from the scene for almost 3 years.

After this win, his school nominated him for the Championship Trophy at Colorado. He felt honoured to be considered for this opportunity. He very well knew that the world's federal athletics committee gathered there every year to pick up fresh talented youngsters and groom them for world championships. When Osborne resumed back to school after his summer holidays, he was given a grand welcome by his teachers and classmates. That day, in the middle of a lecture, Osborne received a message saying that his principal wanted to meet him after the class.

As soon as the classes were over, Osborne proceeded towards the Principal's cabin. He knocked on the cabin door before entering. The principal sat there speaking to a person. Osborne first greeted the principal. His principal was a wise and intellectual person who always took a keen interest in his students' progress. He said that he had good news for Osborne. Before that, he introduced Osborne to the person sitting opposite to him. "Meet Ron, he has been appointed by the Sports committee as your official trainer and coach. He has been specially selected to groom you for the Colorado Championship. You can take your own time to practice during school hours. I will relax the academic rules for you. I wish you all the best in your endeavour." Saying this, he pointed towards Ron

Harvey, and said, "He is all yours".

The very first sight of Ron reminded Osborne of his daddy. Ron stepped out of the principal's cabin, his hands clasped around Osborne's arms. He just said, "From what I understand, you do not need a coach at this instant. You are a born athlete. However, maybe you need a friend at this stage to encourage and support you just like your father did." These words of Ron were enough to lift the spirits of Osborne. His frank attitude instantly won the faith of Osborne. The next day Ron met Osborne at 7 AM in the morning at the school ground. Ron had made a fitness schedule for Osborne. Daily, he used to make Osborne run at least 5 km and set a time on his stopwatch.

The next day he used to set a lesser time to check if Osborne was improving. Osborne had never been so serious regarding practice sessions before. Ron guided him to show faith in his abilities and boosted his confidence. At the same time, he also taught him to gather the courage to meet failures in life. Osborne was a changed person after a few days. The bond between them was growing each single day. Osborne's mother was extremely delighted seeing her son stepping into a new world.

There were only 2 months to go for the championship when unfortunately Osborne contracted a respiratory infection. His mother was extremely worried because his condition was worsening each single day. It was then that Ron took charge of the situation. He stood by Osborne in this hour of crisis. He served him supplements and fruit juices so that he could recuperate soon. He also consoled his mother and said that her son would be better in a few days. Though the doctors had put forth their opinion that it would take at least a month for him to recover completely, they were taken aback by Osborne's strong willpower and confidence, which cured him of his sickness within 20 days. Just a few days were left for the event.

Though Osborne was discharged from the hospital, he realised that his sickness had thrown him completely out of gear and he needed to retain all the stamina. His hectic sessions began soon thereafter. He started taking energy drinks and indulged in some heavy workout to gain his lost weight. At the same time, he also ran twice the time he used to earlier. Gradually he was back to his normal physique after a few days.

Finally, the big day arrived. Osborne got ready by 6 AM in the morning. His mother kissed him goodbye. Ron had arranged a small private jet for Osborne that would take them to Colorado. It was the flight of the phoenix. Osborne glanced at the sky and thought, "Today is a special day in my life."

It was indeed special when Osborne found himself stranded in the jungle that day. He thought that his mentor Ron might be trapped elsewhere in the forest and desperately tried to search for him. Just then he heard a loud roar. He turned in the direction of the sound. A Jaguar stared at him with bloodshot eyes, just 300 feet away. The Jaguar had tracked down its target. Now it was Osborne's turn to set his target.

In Colorado, the gunshot before the marathon was fired. At the same time, the chase also started in the jungle. Osborne knew that the rough, uneven and rocky path in the jungle was his racetrack today. "But this win would be strictly off-the-records," he jokingly thought. He decided to go for the kill. Initially, Osborne was quick on his feet but his stamina was low due to immense loss of blood. The jaguar was not far behind. He encountered thorny bushes on the way that bore scratches and cuts on his body. Leeches stuck onto his body sucking his blood. But nothing seemed to deter his spirits. He did not know where he was headed to, whether he was penetrating the jungle or finding his way out of it. But he still continued to run because he wanted to live. The jaguar was approaching him at a fast pace. He knew he had to dodge the jaguar at any cost and distract him from its target. So he decided to take the path less travelled. Osborne saw a deep narrow turn sloping downwards; he knew the huge jaguar could not make it through the narrow turn. So he took that way.

After a while, when he looked behind, the jaguar was nowhere to be seen. His commitment to continue running had saved his life. But he still ran; he knew if he stopped now, he could never gather the courage to resume back. He interpreted the jaguar as an opportunity for propelling him to find his way out. Suddenly, he started feeling that he was running on wet muddy ground. Maybe he was approaching a river nearby. He could cross the river and reach the other end, he thought. This could mark the end of his journey. As he ran, what he thought was his final lap; he heard water striking the rocks.

Finally, it was the end of the forest path. But what lay ahead astonished him. A vast stretch of water surrounded him and he realised that he was in the middle of an island, an island covered by dense forest. He finally stopped running. With gasping breath, he erupted into laughter. He could never believe that this is all happening to him. He thought this was the biggest joke in his life. Suddenly a surge of thought ran through his mind that left him baffled. As he looked up at the sky, he remembered those moments when he sat with Ron in the jet on his way to Colorado. These were the moments that he was desperately trying to recollect. Ron was there right beside him in the craft.

After covering a few miles, Ron asked a question to Osborne, "You know Os, why did I teach you how to deal with failures in life," to which Osborne replied, "No." Ron asserted, "You have never come across failures in your life. Neither did my son before you defeated him at the Red Cross Marathon event. Today is indeed going to be a special day for you. I was just waiting for this day; you shattered my son's dreams, and you hurt a father. In your absence, my son Malcolm would deserve to qualify today. I am gonna pick him up on the way. I want to see my son win his third championship. I wish you all the best in your failure. Hope you learn from it." Saying this, he pushed Osborne out of the jet right into the jungle island.

Osborne was feeling more relaxed now. He had finally come to terms with his memoirs. Though he knew that there was one more lap to cross, he courageously geared up. He thought, "Ron, you are definitely a better coach than a father. Otherwise, I would not have reached this far, and your son would not have lost that day. I salute you from the bottom of my heart. I want to make you feel proud. I am on my way. See you soon." Saying this, he jumped into the shallow waters to swim across and reach the boat, which he had spotted not far away from the island to reach the shores. The Final Lap was indeed the longest one & Osborne would cross that too.

21

DESTINY'S CHILD

Mr. and Mrs. Shreenivasan, i.e. Us, came down the building for a stroll holding their boy Shashwat's hand. Shashwat was a loving and adorable boy who was always excited to be with both his parents. His favourite pastime was to go to the building play area where he used to meet his friends and play various games. Kavita aunty was taking a walk nearby and on seeing us gave a surprised look and asked how come both of us were together. Actually, the neighbours knew us too well. We were the super busy couple juggling many roles in this hectic world.

The COVID times had changed everybody's lives. Earlier, both of us used to travel to work, keeping Shashwat at his grandparents' place. He was just 3 years old then. Although he loved spending time with his grandparents who took good care of him, he always yearned to be with his parents. Fortunately, his dreams came true when the pandemic started and everyone started working from home. Initially, it was a bit difficult for us to manage as our jobs demanded a lot of our time. I used to spend time with Shashwat in the afternoon, played with him and gave him good company. His mother used to spend time with him in the evenings. We tried to shuffle our times so that he would not feel alone. But all this was short-lived.

His online school started. He started getting hitched to the laptop more, and his mother was busy with his school and learning. With the pandemic peaking at regular intervals, it was difficult to have maids regularly at home considering the restrictions imposed. Half the time was spent cleaning home, cooking food, managing his school and our work. What seemed to be a blessing for us earlier started turning the tide. Shashwat saw us grappling with multiple things and realised that he would not be able to spend much time with us in the day. In the evenings too, when the other kids would come along with both their parents to the garden, he stared at them in jealousy.

Before the pandemic, even though time was less, it was quality time spent with him, but now even when they had all the time, it just went in vain. Job stress started taking a toll on our mental lives. Daily arguments over trivial matters related to home started growing into full-fledged abusive fights. It had a bad impression on Shashwat at first, but then he started getting used to it. With late calls happening at work, even he could not listen to bedtime stories from us that he used to while we used to commute to work. We started sleeping in different rooms. Some days he would be with his mom, while on other days he used to be with me. I used to feel sad for him but didn't know what to do. As offices became more flexible offering extended work-from-home benefits, the pain only grew more. That was our story.

Now let me come back to the present times which have changed.

He was now a 7-year-old boy. I started pampering him more. His mother also did the same. Suddenly things changed. You would wonder how. It was he who changed us. I gave up my full-time job to spend some quality time with him. We thought all these years of struggle should stop somehow, so both of us took part-time jobs with sufficient time to spare for the family. Slowly things started getting back to normal. We both sorted out our differences and stopped having big fights at home. Whatever came up too was discussed when Shashwat was not around. Shashwat slowly started becoming happier.

That day I was cuddling him in bed when his mother called him to get ready. He instantly got up and ran. After wearing his favourite t-shirt, he glanced at me to check my expression. He then waved his hand at me to come along. I got up from bed and got ready. We held his hand and took him down the building. Kavita aunty surprisingly gazed at our hands and then muttered something to herself and went away. We sat there watching Shashwat play in the sand, although he was playing alone. He was so excited that today both of us got time to spend with him together. As the sun set and it turned dark, we came back upstairs. The smile on his face was palpable. He came down to both of us and said 'Mamma Pappa please be like this forever and stay with me. Never leave me alone'. Tears started rolling in our eyes.

The other day, there was a medical drive being carried out in our society. The doorbell rang at our home. I opened the door. The person standing outside asked for the number of members at home. I said 3. He asked me to call everyone. I called my wife and kid. He again asked, "Can you please share the family members count?" and I said 3. He looked baffled.

When I saw his register, he simply wrote 2 and left. There was a reason Kavita aunty was whispering something to herself when she saw us in the garden. It was not only her, but all the others too, who maintained a distance from us. For them, Shashwat was gone. He was inside the safe doors of heaven. But he was still with us; no one believed this. The day he died due to asphyxiation, we were so puzzled. Both of us were at home then, and none of us realised. We didn't even get the time to take him to the hospital. That incident took their child far away from them. We came back home from his funeral, sat there in absolute silence. His memories could not be erased so easily, and slowly he came back to life for us from those memories.

Both of us were able to see him, so we considered him to be real. That day we decided, "Let's give our time to our kid."

The precious formative years that we missed spending with him were indeed valuable, so we started a life afresh even though it was only imaginary for him. Shashwat always yearned to be with us, so he returned, and we committed that this time we would not make the same mistake again, so we started spending more and more time with him.

Let's strive to spend good quality time with our kids amidst all this chaos in the world of smartphones and fake luxuries. Let them not dwell in laptops, tablets, or social media when we spend our lives busy shopping online, nor let them be exposed to mutual differences and fights at home. For we will not get another chance as the Shreenivasans.

22

THE BRAVE AND THE MIGHTY

Not so long ago, there was a vast jungle inhabited by many wild animals and dense plant species. Streams and rivers flowed through the jungle. The days were lit with sunshine and filled with the beautiful sounds of chirping birds and flowing water, while fireflies illuminated the nights, surrounded by buzzing insects. Most of the animals that were active during the day took rest, and it was then that the night predators hunted their prey in the quiet of the night. But what was most striking about the jungle was that it was ruled by a ferocious, mighty lion. The Beast never came out into the open and always remained in his shelter cave, so no one had the chance to catch a glimpse of him. The animals of the jungle were not allowed to talk about the Beast. They believed he was the protector of the jungle.

The Beast was an animal of principles. He never allowed any harm to come to anyone in the jungle in any form. He knew how to restore balance and set rules for the other wild animals, ensuring they did not cross the limits. So every animal in the jungle was happy under his rule, though they were equally fearful of him. The Beast was known to have his own unique style of feasting. He did not go out hunting for his prey; instead, his prey would surrender to him. This would only happen when the Lion was actually hungry. Rules were set about whose turn it would be to feed the lion. On the day they would surrender, these animals were so anxious to see this legend and its splendor that they would forget they would never return. They considered this to be some sort of blessing. The Beast would provide them with the best meal of their life that day, tailored to their tastes, before feasting on their soft flesh after asking them to rest. It was said that these animals did not even feel pain when the Beast bit them, as he cast a magical spell that transported them to a different world.

There were a few lucky ones who, despite having surrendered to the Beast, still made it back unharmed and alive. No one knew why they returned. Could the Beast be kind enough to let anyone go for no reason? Or were these animals special? Some of these lucky ones included a rabbit, a chimpanzee, a peacock, and a deer. Upon returning, these animals started to keep to themselves and did not mingle with the other creatures. When the other animals approached them to learn how they managed to escape the Beast's claws, they attributed it to destiny. Other animals observed these special ones and noticed that something changed in them over time. The sensitive rabbit, who usually listened for the smallest of sounds and fled in fear, suddenly started ignoring those sounds. The deer, which usually traveled in a group, began strolling alone. The chimpanzee, though wild and naughty, became a lot more composed, while the peacock, whose graceful dance mesmerized any audience and was mostly found atop the trees, came down freely and roamed the jungle. All of these animals became braver than before.

A few months passed. Slowly, these special animals who returned after meeting the Beast began disappearing from the jungle one by one. When they were not seen around, the others presumed they had made a deal with the Beast to spend a few more days freely before surrendering. So, they assumed they were gone. One day, it was the buffalo's turn to satiate the hunger of the Beast. He secretly wished he had more time to spend with his family. Upon arriving at the doors of the Beast, he pleaded with the mighty creature to give him some more time. The Beast made the buffalo understand that there are laws of the jungle that prohibit him from doing so. But the buffalo asked how the rabbit, peacock, deer, and chimpanzee had come back to spend some time before eventually returning to the Beast. Upon hearing this, the Beast said that was just a rumor spread by him, which was actually not true. The buffalo asked him why he had spread this rumor. The Beast explained that he did so to convince the jungle animals. The truth was that those animals were actually on some secret mission, dispatched by the Beast for that purpose. The buffalo gave up hope and surrendered to the Beast.

One day, the animals sent on the mission—who had disappeared from the jungle—appeared out of nowhere. They went to their homes and met their families. They had serious discussions with others in the jungle too. When the Beast realized these animals were back, he summoned them. They came to meet him, and the Beast welcomed them back. He asked how their journey to the other side of the jungle had been and apprehended them by asking what took them so long to return. The journey was rough for each one of them, they said. The Beast had teleported them to a different time where some of the animals had already gone extinct. The special animals crossed all the stages of civilization during this journey.

Then, he popped up the million-dollar question—the purpose of sending those animals to a different era. "Have you found someone mightier than the Beast?" they replied, "Yes." The Beast asked each one of them who it was, and a common answer emerged: "The Man."

The Man hunts the Beast, tames him, and can kill him too, they said. The Beast might be strong, but he is not clever enough for Man. Upon hearing this, the Beast was disappointed.

All the aura, charisma, valor, and strength he possessed held no value outside the jungle. After many years, he realized that he had the wrong notion of being the king of the world and that he would always rule all time. However, after hearing from them, he understood that his power was only limited to the jungle for a finite time. The glory would soon fade away.

"I give you back your freedom," he said. "You are free." The special animals were surprised.

No one knew that this Beast had the unique power to cast himself upon those he wished. Therefore, the animals who came back to visit the Beast unharmed were braver than before, but only on the condition that they offered their duty to the king. Inside the bodies and minds of these animals lived the Beast, who had sent them on a mission. What these animals saw was the hard reality of the future. Man would tame animals as pets. They saw animals being slaughtered harshly and consumed as food by these men. In some places, like circuses, even mighty animals like lions, tigers, and elephants were made to behave like puppets, mimicking the actions of men. They also saw men riding some of these animals—like horses, elephants, and camels—just for leisure. The thick fur made from animal skin was, nevertheless, the same manner of exploitation. Outside the jungle, not just the lion, but all the other animals too had no chance of survival and free will. Now these men were encroaching upon the jungles as well.

The Beast dared to know whether his strength matched that of any of the others living. But the biggest mistake he made was sending his fellow animals to find out the actual truth. These fellow animals, who came back after seeing the outside world, were no longer in awe of the Beast but were, in fact, more fearful of Man. They spread this news throughout the jungle before they came to meet the Beast. This not only cost him the respect the other animals had for him all this time but also caused them to lose their fear of him.

What the Beast didn't know was that he was, in fact, the strongest for his time and place. He possessed powers that no one else did, but his insecurities eclipsed his mind, making him weaker and eventually costing him his life, which was now filled with fear. He failed to realize that he was not responsible for anyone's distorted perception of him. Instead, he should have invoked his wrath and fury to justify his place and earn the respect he duly deserved as a king.

So, don't chase competition. Stand firm in your own light and truth.

23

THE OLD DICTIONARY

My grandson was an English Literature professor, and he used to teach at MIT. It was the year 2087. English was no longer the language it had been earlier. Although mostly adapted from British English, it had developed its unique pattern. The accents were different, the verbiage was different, but all in all, the language was still the same.

However, after 2048, a scholar from England thought of modifying the dictionary. Some words like "original," and "natural," , were all removed, considering the fact that nothing was left original at that time. Whether it was food that was processed or medicines made of only chemical ingredients, nothing remained untouched. Breakfast and lunch were separate earlier. Now, people hardly have time to have one proper meal in a day. There is cut-throat competition everywhere. So, breakfast and lunch are now brunch. There are no longer restaurants serving breakfast in the morning.

Given that the city, which works all day, rarely sleeps, restaurants and shops now open after 11 AM and remain open until 3 AM.The word "slow" is gone, as everything is quick these days. Kids are not taught opposites in school where they know they have a choice of taking things slow. It's only quick action, quick studies. The age is of the Fast and Furious. As we humans didn't nurture our environment well enough, the forests disappeared. So did all the wild animals. Most of them became extinct, barring a few domestic animals like cats and dogs that stayed close to the human population. The younger generation never knew what it was like to go to a jungle and explore wildlife.

Most importantly, the mediums that were so easily accessible to everyone, i.e., newspapers and books, disappeared too. There were only online editions available. The joy of having a book in hand and slowly turning down the pages was no longer felt by the younger generations. People were more serious these days, scared all the time, thinking when a missile might come down from somewhere and drop at their place, as in the last few years, there have been frequent conflicts leading to the rise of more and more war-torn regions. See the irony, there were only stories of wars being circulated everywhere, and that was the only point of discussion left between everyone. Money was no longer paper currency. Seeing that books no longer existed and paper currency was gone, no one knew what the word "paper" meant anymore.

Everything was digital, including memories. People don't remember anyone by their names; they have an alphanumeric code these days that flash in the air when they pass each other. What an awesome technology. So, the phrase "Excuse me" also vanished. People no longer used to call strangers saying "Excuse Me"; they used to call them by their pseudonyms/codes, which were actually identifiers and not real names. Kids no longer used to play in playgrounds; they didn't even know playgrounds existed. There were only courts everywhere, like a badminton court, tennis court, cricket or football court, etc. AI reached another level, and there was an AI bot sanctioned by the government to everyone who was born, and this AI bot remained throughout the lifespan of the person. This AI Bot had the DNA of the human infused in it; human brains shrank to a minimal size as all the logical and analytical questioning of the mind was replaced by AI Bot. Emotions no longer had a place, so relationships slowly lost their meaning. What was perceived by the mind was no longer quantified.

At first, there were a lot of museums everywhere; in the early times, I remember museums used to have artifacts that were hundreds of years old. With rapid innovation happening so frequently, every two years things were being moved into the Archives of the Museum, and there was no space left there anymore. So gradually, even the museum made its way out. People didn't know directions, like East-West, North-South. Navigation satellites and GPS Maps were encoded in every smart device, and wherever you wanted to go, your AI bot would automatically sense it and take you there without you even looking at Maps and driving in those directions.

Forget driving — there were only self-driving cars. What a pitiful life it was. This generation has not seen anything yet, but claims they are much more ahead of their times.

Leaving all this aside and returning to the main story, which correlates with everything I have mentioned, my grandson one day found an old dictionary in my old warehouse. It was torn, and the ink had almost faded, but he painstakingly transcribed every word from the old dictionary into a digital format. Today, he is going to discuss that dictionary as a part of his lecture and I am so excited for him, as I helped him retrieve every single word that no longer had its origins in the new age. Today, the younger generation will at least learn what life was like before, and I wish someone would do more research, propagate the idea, and bring about a fresh lease of life into old times.

24

MATCH MADE IN HEAVEN

How beautiful are the wedding rituals in our culture! From the blessing of rings and the exchange of vows to the prayers recited for the couple, each moment is filled with divine significance. When the candles are lit, they signify the amalgamation of the couple's lives from that moment onward. The priest welcomes the congregation, and the couple makes their promises in front of God. It is said that during these wedding rituals, when hymns are recited in the name of the Lord, holy angels appear from heaven to witness the event and cast their blessings upon the couple.

I was one of the angels who appeared to witness the wedding of Stephanie and James. While the other angels who accompanied me were busy showering love on the couple, my attention drifted outside the church, to the opposite side of the road. I felt deep vibes of spellbinding love emanating from that place. But before I reach there, let me tell you another story.

This is the story of Charlotte and Henry. Henry was an orphan raised in an orphanage. As a child, he often watched carpenters working in the orphanage, building small tables and desks for the kids to use in school. He would help them cut and shape wooden blocks. The main carpenter, Dominic, was very fond of Henry and got the headmistress's permission to take him along on carpentry jobs outside the orphanage. Henry enjoyed these trips and looked forward to them.

One day, while accompanying Dominic to a house, Henry met a small girl named Charlotte. She had twinkling eyes, a tiny ponytail, and wore a pink velvet skirt with frills. She was dancing outside. When she saw him, she ran inside at first but later came out and asked him to play with her. Her father worked in the postal department outside the city, and only her mother was at home to care for her. Charlotte was mischievous and full of energy.

Every day, Henry eagerly awaited the moment when Dominic would take him to Charlotte's house. They played together, and Charlotte insisted that Henry accompany her to school and stay for meals. Over time, Henry became like a family member, and he grew fond of her.

After a month, the carpentry work at Charlotte's house was completed. As a farewell gesture, Henry made her a couple of wooden dolls and gave them to her. Though the work was done, he continued to visit her on her way to school and in the evenings to play. Their bond grew stronger with each passing day. Years went by, and their relationship remained steadfast. Henry became a full-time carpenter, working at various houses, while Charlotte grew into a beautiful young woman. One day, Henry proposed to her, and she accepted. It was the happiest day of his life.

But their happiness was short-lived. News of Charlotte's father's passing soon spread. Henry, who was out of town for work, returned to find Charlotte's house locked and empty. He initially thought they might have gone to the church, but days turned into weeks, and there was no sign of them. None of the neighbors knew where Charlotte and her mother had gone. Devastated, Henry felt abandoned. This was a time before mobile phones, and communication was limited to distant telephone booths. Months passed without any news, and Henry tried to move on, believing that fate had other plans.

One day, Charlotte's school friend, Mary, met Henry at church and revealed what had happened. Charlotte had taken a job in the postal department where her father had worked. With no one else to care for her family, she had moved away but had left a message with Mary: she promised to return for Henry one day. Unfortunately, Mary had been away visiting her grandmother and only delivered the message much later. Upon hearing this, Henry decided to wait for Charlotte.

Three years passed, but Charlotte did not return. Growing impatient, Henry resolved to search for her. He packed some beautiful dresses for her and set off, taking a bus from his town. Along the way, he stopped to deliver wooden consignments for Dominic's contact.

When he arrived, he found bulldozers demolishing the block. The house had been built on illegal land, and the civic authorities had ordered its destruction. Dominic's relative, who lived there, was crying inconsolably.

As Henry tried to console her, she pointed to a carton inside the house and pleaded with him to retrieve it. Without hesitation, Henry stepped inside to get the carton. Suddenly, the roof collapsed as the bulldozer struck the back wall, trapping Henry beneath the rubble. As Henry lay there in pain, he heard church bells ringing across the road and saw a beautiful couple arriving for their wedding. The sight overwhelmed him with emotion. Moments later, he took his last breath. Since no one in the town knew him, and he was an orphan, he was buried in the cemetery outside the church.

But Henry's story did not end there. As his soul lingered, he noticed the grave next to his and read the name: Charlotte Moses. In that moment, Charlotte's soul embraced Henry's, and their reunion, though delayed, was finally complete. It turned out that Charlotte had set out to meet Henry just days before her death. Her mother had been pressuring her to marry someone she did not love, so she had abandoned her job and left behind anything that could help trace her. She, too, had died an orphan, and by divine providence, she was buried next to Henry. Their destinies had always been intertwined. If not in life, then in death, they were meant to be together. The angel, witnessing this union of souls, showered blessings upon them before returning to heaven.

To the Seasons, each holding its own story

www.ingramcontent.com/pod-product-compliance
Lightning Source LLC
Chambersburg PA
CBHW030814170726
47995CB00013B/852